THE BEAST FROM THE EAST

ALL-NEW! ALL-TERRIFYING!

Goosebumps®

NOW WITH BONUS FEATURES!
LOOK IN THE BACK OF THE BOOK FOR
EXCLUSIVE AUTHOR INTERVIEWS AND MORE.

THE BEAST FROM THE EAST

R.L. STINE

SCHOLASTIC INC.
New York Toronto London Auckland Sydney
Mexico City New Delhi Hong Kong Buenos Aires

ISBN 0-439-72403-1

The *Goosebumps* book series created by Parachute Press, Inc.
Published by Scholastic Inc.
SCHOLASTIC, GOOSEBUMPS,
and associated logos are trademarks and/or registered
trademarks of Scholastic Inc.

12 11 10   8 9 10/0

Printed in the U.S.A.   40

THE BEAST FROM THE EAST

1

When I was a really little girl, my mom would tuck me into bed at night. She would whisper, "Good night, Ginger. Good night. Don't let the bedbugs bite."

I didn't know what bedbugs were. I pictured fat red bugs with big eyes and spidery legs, crawling under the sheet. Just thinking about them made me itchy all over.

After Mom kissed me on the forehead and left, Dad would step into my room and sing to me. Very softly. The same song every night. "The Teddy Bears' Picnic."

I don't know why he thought that song made a good lullaby. It was about going into the woods and finding hundreds and hundreds of bears.

The song gave me the shivers. What were the bears eating at their picnic? Children?

After Dad kissed me on the forehead and left the room, I'd be itching and shaking for hours.

Then I'd have nightmares about bedbugs and bears.

Until a few years ago, I was afraid to go into the woods.

I'm twelve now, and I'm not scared any longer.

At least, I wasn't scared until our family camping trip this summer. That's when I discovered that there are a lot scarier creatures than bears in the woods!

But I guess I'd better begin at the beginning.

The first thing I remember about our camping trip is Dad yelling at my brothers. I have two ten-year-old brothers — Pat and Nat. You guessed it. They're twins.

Lucky me — huh?

Pat and Nat aren't just twins. They're identical twins. They look so much alike, they confuse *each other*!

They are both short and skinny. They both have round faces and big brown eyes. They both wear their brown hair parted in the middle and straight down the sides. They both wear baggy, faded jeans and black-and-red skater T-shirts with slogans no one can understand.

There is only one way to tell Pat from Nat or Nat from Pat. You have to ask them who they are!

I remember that our camping trip began on a beautiful, sunny day. The air smelled piney and fresh. Twigs and dead leaves crackled under our shoes as we followed a twisting path through the woods.

Dad led the way. He carried the tent over his shoulder, and he had a bulging backpack on his back. Mom followed him. She was also loaded down with stuff we needed.

The path led through a grassy clearing. The sun felt hot on my face. My backpack began to feel heavy. I wondered how much deeper into the woods Mom and Dad wanted to go.

Pat and Nat followed behind us. Dad kept turning around to yell at them. We all had to yell at Pat and Nat. Otherwise, they never seemed to hear us. They only heard each other.

Why was Dad yelling?

Well, for one thing, Nat kept disappearing. Nat likes to climb trees. If he sees a good tree, he climbs it. I think he's part chimpanzee.

I tell him that as often as I can. Then he scratches his chest and makes chimp noises. He thinks he's really funny.

So there we were, hiking through the woods. And every time we turned around, Nat would be up a tree somewhere. It was slowing us down. So Dad had to yell at him.

Then Dad had to yell at Pat because of his Game Boy. "I told you not to bring that thing!" Dad shouted. Dad is big and broad, kind of like a bear. And he has a booming voice.

It doesn't do him much good. Pat and Nat never listen to him.

Pat walked along, eyes on his Game Boy, his fingers hammering the controls.

"Why are we hiking in the woods?" Dad asked him. "You could be home in your room doing that. Put it away, Pat, and check out the scenery."

"I can't, Dad," Pat protested. "I can't quit now. I'm on Level Six! I've never made it to Level Six before!"

"There goes a chipmunk," Mom chimed in, pointing. Mom is the wildlife guide. She points out everything that moves.

Pat didn't raise his eyes from his Game Boy.

"Where's Nat?" Dad demanded, his eyes searching the clearing.

"Up here, Dad," Nat called. I shielded my eyes with one hand and saw him on a high branch of a tall oak tree.

"Get down from there!" Dad shouted. "That branch won't hold you!"

"Hey — I made it to Level Seven!" Pat declared, fingering frantically.

"Look — two bunny rabbits!" Mom cried. "See them in the tall grass?"

"Let's keep walking," I groaned. "It's too hot here." I wanted to get out of the clearing and back under the cool shade of the trees.

"Ginger is the only sensible one," Dad said, shaking his head.

"Ginger is a freak!" Nat called, sliding down from the oak tree.

We made our way through the woods. I don't know how long we walked. It was so beautiful! So peaceful. Beams of sunlight poked through the high branches, making the ground sparkle.

I found myself humming that song about the bears in the woods. I don't know what made it pop into my head. Dad hadn't sung it to me in years and years.

We stopped for lunch by a clear, trickling stream. "This would make a nice camping spot," Mom suggested. "We can set up the tent on the grass here by the shore."

Mom and Dad started to unpack the equipment and set up the tent. I helped them. Pat and Nat threw stones into the stream. Then they got into a wrestling match and tried to shove each other into the water.

"Take them into the woods," Dad instructed me. "Try to lose them — okay?"

He was joking, of course.

He had no way of knowing that Pat, Nat, and I would soon be lost for real — with little hope of ever returning.

2

"What do you want to do?" Nat demanded. He had picked up a thin tree branch to use as a walking stick. Pat kept slapping at it, trying to make Nat stumble.

We had followed the stream for a while. I saw a million tiny, silver minnows swimming near the surface. Now we were making our own path through the tangle of trees, low shrubs, and rocks.

"Hide-and-seek!" Pat declared. He slapped Nat. "You're It!"

Nat slapped him back. "You're It."

"You're It!"

"You're It!"

"You're It!"

The slaps kept getting harder.

"I'll be It!" I cried. Anything to keep them from murdering each other. "Hurry. Go hide. But don't go too far."

I leaned against a tree, shut my eyes, and

started to count to one hundred. I could hear them scampering into the trees.

After thirty, I counted by tens. I didn't want to give them too big a head start. "Ready or not, here I come!" I called.

I found Pat after only a few minutes. He had crouched behind a large white mound of sand. He thought he was hidden. But I spotted his brown hair poking up over the top of the sand.

I tagged him easily.

Nat was harder to find. He had climbed a tree, of course. He was way up at the top, completely hidden by thick clumps of green leaves.

I never would have found him if he hadn't spit on me.

"Get down, creep!" I shouted angrily. I waved a fist up at him. "You're disgusting! Get down — right now!"

He giggled and peered down at me. "Did I hit you?"

I didn't answer. I waited for him to climb down to the ground. Then I rubbed a handful of dried leaves in his face until he was sputtering and choking.

Just a typical Wald family hide-and-seek game.

After that, we chased a squirrel through the woods. The poor thing kept glancing back at us as if he didn't believe we were chasing after him. He finally got tired of the race and scurried up a tall pine tree.

I glanced around. The trees in this part of the woods grew close together. Their leaves blocked most of the sunlight. The air felt cooler here. In their shade, it was nearly as dark as evening.

"Let's go back," I suggested. "Mom and Dad might be getting worried."

The boys didn't argue. "Which way?" Nat asked.

I glanced around, making a complete circle with my eyes. "Uh . . . that way." I pointed. I was guessing. But I felt ninety-nine percent sure.

"Are you sure?" Pat asked. He eyed me suspiciously. I could see he was a little worried. Pat didn't like the outdoors as much as Nat and me.

"Sure I'm sure," I told him.

I led the way. They followed close behind. They had both picked up walking sticks. After we had walked a few minutes, they started fighting a duel with them.

I ignored them. I had my own worries. I wasn't sure we were walking in the right direction. In fact, I felt totally turned around.

"Hey — there's the stream!" I cried happily.

I immediately felt better. We weren't lost. I had picked the right direction.

Now all we had to do was follow the stream back to the clearing where we had set up camp.

I began to hum again. The boys tossed their sticks into the stream. We began to jog along the grassy shore.

"Whoa!" I cried out when my left boot started to sink. I nearly fell into a deep mud patch. I pulled my hiking boot up. Soaked in wet, brown mud up over the ankle.

Pat and Nat thought that was a riot. They laughed and slapped each other high fives.

I growled at them, but I didn't waste any words. They're both hopeless. So totally immature.

Now I couldn't wait to get back to camp and clean the thick mud off my boot. We jogged along the shore, then cut through the skinny, white-trunked trees and into the clearing.

"Mom! Dad!" I called, hurrying over the grass. "We're back!"

I stopped so short, both boys tumbled into me.

My eyes searched the clearing.

"Mom? Dad?"

They were gone.

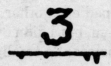

3

"They left us!" Pat exclaimed. He ran frantically around the clearing. "Mom! Dad!"

"Earth to Pat," Nat called. He waved his hand in front of Pat's face. "We're in the wrong place, you wimp."

"Nat is right," I replied, glancing around. There were no footprints, no tent markers. We were in a different clearing.

"I thought you knew the way, Ginger," Pat complained. "Didn't they teach you anything at that nature camp?"

Nature camp! Last summer my parents forced me to spend two weeks at an "Explore the Great Outdoors" camp. I got poison ivy the first day. After that, I didn't listen to anything the counselors said.

Now I wished I had.

"We should have left markers on the trees," I said, "to find our way back."

"*Now* you think of it?" Nat groaned, rolling his

10

eyes. He picked up a long, crooked stick and waved it in my face.

"Give me that," I ordered.

Nat handed me the stick. Yellow sap oozed onto my palm. It smelled sour.

"Gross!" I shouted. I tossed the stick away. I rubbed my hands on my jeans. But the yellow stain wouldn't come off my palm.

That's weird, I thought. I wondered what the stuff was. I definitely didn't like it on my skin.

"Let's follow the stream," I suggested. "Mom and Dad can't be too far."

I tried to sound calm. But I was totally twisted around. In fact, I had no idea where we were.

We headed out of the clearing and back to the shore. The sun fell lower in the sky. It prickled the back of my neck.

Pat and Nat tossed pebbles into the water. After a few minutes, they tossed them at each other.

I ignored them. At least they weren't throwing anything at me.

As we walked along, the air became cooler. The path grew narrower.

The water turned dark and murky. Silvery-blue fish snapped at the air. The skinny branches of the tall trees reached down toward us.

A feeling of dread swept over me. Nat and Pat grew quiet. They actually stopped picking on each other.

"I don't remember any of these bushes near our campsite," Pat said nervously. He pointed to a short, squat plant. Its strange blue leaves looked like open umbrellas stacked one on top of the other. "Are you sure we're going the right way?"

By now I was sure we *weren't* headed in the right direction. I didn't remember those strange bushes, either.

Then we heard a noise on the other side of the shrubs.

"Maybe that's Mom and Dad!" Pat exclaimed.

We pushed our way through the plants. And ran into another *deserted* clearing.

I glanced around. This grassy field was enormous. Large enough for a hundred tents.

My heart hammered against my chest.

We stood on rust-colored grass. It stuck up over my ankle. A clump of gigantic purple cabbage plants grew to our right.

"This place is cool!" Nat cried. "Everything is so big."

To me, the clearing wasn't cool at all. It gave me the creeps.

Strange trees surrounded us on all sides. Their branches shot out at right angles to the trunk. They resembled stairs going up and up and up. Up into the clouds.

They were the tallest trees I'd ever seen. And perfect for climbing.

Red moss clung to the branches. Yellow gourds hung from braided vines, swaying in the air.

Where were we? This looked like a weird jungle — not the woods! Why were all the trees and plants so strange?

A knot formed in the pit of my stomach.

Where was our clearing? Where were Mom and Dad?

Nat jogged over to a tree. "I'm climbing up," he said.

"No, you don't," I protested. I rushed over and pulled his arm from the branch.

The red moss rubbed against my palm. My skin turned red where I touched it. Now I had a yellow-and-red design on my hand.

What's going on here? I wondered.

Before I could show my hand to my brothers, the tree started to shake.

"Whoa! Watch out!" I cried.

A small furry animal jumped out of the branches and landed at my feet. I had never seen anything like it before. It was the size of a chipmunk, brown all over except for a white patch around one eye.

It had a bushy tail and floppy ears like a bunny. And two big front teeth like a beaver. Its flat nose twitched. It stared at me with gray eyes, round with fear. I watched it scurry away.

"What was that?" Pat asked.

I shrugged. I wondered what other kinds of weird creatures lived in these woods.

13

"I'm kind of scared," Pat admitted, huddling close to me.

I felt scared too. But I knew I was the big sister. So I told him everything was okay.

Then I glanced down. "Nat! Pat!" I shouted. "Look!"

My muddy boot stood inside a footprint three times the size of mine. No — even bigger. What kind of animal had a footprint that huge?

A bear? A giant gorilla?

I didn't have time to think about it.

The ground started to tremble.

"Do you feel that?" I asked my brothers.

"It's Dad!" Pat shouted.

It definitely was not Dad. He's a big guy. But no way could he make the ground shake that way!

I heard grumbles and growls from somewhere in the distance. And then a roar. Twigs and branches snapped loudly in the air.

All three of us gasped as a tall beast stomped through the trees. It was huge. So tall that its head touched the middle branches.

It had a narrow, pointy head over a long neck. Its eyes shone like bright green marbles. Shaggy blue fur covered every part of its body. Its long, furry tail thumped heavily on the ground.

The weirdest creature I'd ever seen in my life!

The beast entered the far side of the clearing.

I sucked in my breath as it drew closer. Close

enough for me to see its long snout. Its nostrils flared in and out as it sniffed the air.

My brothers hung back, hiding behind me. We huddled together. Trembling.

The beast opened its mouth. Two rows of sharp, yellow teeth rose up from purple gums. One long, jagged fang slid down over the creature's chin.

I crouched on my hands and knees. Pulled my brothers down with me.

The beast spun around in circles. It sniffed the air and wiggled its hairy, pointed ears. Had it smelled us? Was it searching for us?

I couldn't think. I couldn't move.

The beast turned its ugly head. It stared at me. It saw me.

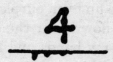

4

My eyes on the creature, I grabbed my brothers by their T-shirts. I dragged them behind some of the huge cabbage plants.

The beast stayed on the other side of the clearing, sniffing the air. It stomped back and forth, sniffing hard. The ground seemed to shake each time one of its furry paws hit the ground. I could feel Nat and Pat shiver with fear.

The beast turned away from us.

Whew! I thought. It hasn't seen us. I bit my bottom lip and held onto Pat and Nat.

"*Argggh,*" the beast grunted. It dropped to all fours. It pressed its snout to the ground and crept along, making loud snuffling noises.

I didn't tell Pat or Nat what I was thinking. The beast hadn't seen us — but there was no way we could keep it from smelling us.

Its long tail swished back and forth. The tail banged against the trees. Gourds fell to the ground.

The beast crawled into the center of the clearing. Closer.

I dug my fingernails into my palm.

Turn around, beast, I prayed. Go back into the woods. The blue creature stopped. It sniffed again. And then it turned. It began to creep in our direction.

I swallowed. Hard. My mouth suddenly felt so dry.

The creature's tail pushed against one of the cabbage plants near us. The leaves rustled.

"Get down!" I whispered, shoving my brothers. We stretched out flat on the ground.

The beast stopped a few feet from our hiding place.

Its tail brushed my arm. The fur felt rough and scratchy.

I jerked my arm away. Could he feel me? Was I like a tiny animal to him? One he could pick up and squeeze the way my brothers teased our dog?

The beast rose up on its hind legs and sniffed. It towered over the cabbage plant. It had to be at least eight feet tall!

It picked at its fur with a clawed thumb — and placed whatever it found in his mouth.

A pleased grin formed under its twitching snout. It peered around the clearing.

Don't look down, I prayed. Don't see us.

My body tensed.

The creature growled and ran its long tongue

over its fang. Then it tromped off into the trees.

I let out a sigh of relief.

"We'd better wait a few minutes," I told my brothers. I counted to one hundred. Then I crawled out from behind the plant. No sign of the creature.

But then I felt the earth shake.

"Oh, no!" I gasped. "Here it comes again!"

5

The beast's enormous blue head bobbed up between the trees. How had it come back so fast? And from the other direction?

We scrambled back to our hiding place behind the huge cabbage plant.

"We have to get away from here," I whispered. "If it keeps searching back and forth, it's bound to find us."

"How do we get away?" Nat demanded.

I picked up a gourd from the ground. "I'll throw this gourd. The beast will turn its head to see what the noise is. Then we'll run — in the other direction."

"But, what if it sees us? What if it chases us?" Nat asked. He didn't seem happy about my plan.

Nat and Pat exchanged nervous glances.

"Yeah. What if it runs faster than us?" Pat demanded.

"It won't," I said. I was bluffing. But my brothers didn't know that.

I peeked over the top of the cabbage. The creature stood closer than ever. It sniffed the air, its pink snout coiling like a snake.

I glanced at the gourd in my hand, then brought my arm back, ready to throw.

"Wait!" Pat whispered. "Look!"

My arm froze where it was. Another beast had tromped into the clearing.

And another.

And another.

I gulped. More blue beasts clomped into the clearing.

No way could we make a run for it now.

The enormous creatures tromped around the clearing. They growled and grunted to each other.

One stopped and jabbered loudly in a deep and gravelly voice. The folds of hairless skin under its chin wobbled back and forth.

"Look at them all!" Nat murmured. "There must be at least two dozen."

A small beast jogged into the clearing. Its fur shone a brighter blue than the rest. It stood only about three feet tall.

Was it a child? A young beast?

The tiny beast placed its short, pink snout on the ground and sniffed. Dirt and dried-up bits of leaves stuck to its snout.

"It looks hungry," Pat whispered.

"Shhh!" I warned.

The tiny beast glanced up eagerly. In our direction.

It *did* look hungry. But for what?

I held my breath.

The small beast suddenly scooped a gourd off the ground. It shoved the whole thing into its mouth and crunched down. Yellow juice squirted between its lips and soaked down its shaggy blue fur.

It eats fruit! I cheered silently. That was a good sign. Maybe they are vegetarians, I thought. Maybe they don't eat meat.

I knew that most wild animals ate only one type of food. Either meat, or else fruits and vegetables.

Except for bears, I suddenly remembered. Bears will eat both.

A large beast thudded over to the kid. It yanked the little creature to its feet and began jabbering angrily at it. It dragged the kid back toward the woods.

The beast with the hairless folds of skin stepped into the center of the clearing.

"*Grrugh!*" It snorted at the others. It waved a furry paw in a circle. It waved and grunted and jabbered.

The other creatures nodded and grunted to one another. They seemed to understand each other. They seemed to be grunting some kind of language.

The big beast gave a final grunt. The other creatures turned back toward the woods. They spread out and began to creep silently into the trees. I felt the earth trembling under the pounding of their feet. Twigs and leaves crackled and cracked.

In a few seconds, they had vanished. The clearing stood empty.

I let out another long sigh of relief.

"What are they doing, anyway?" Pat asked.

Nat wiped sweat off his forehead. "They act as if they're searching for something," he answered. "Hunting."

I swallowed hard.

I knew what they were hunting for.

They were hunting for *us*.

And now there were so many of them. Spreading out in every direction.

We don't stand a chance, I realized.

They're going to catch us.

And then what?

6

I stood up slowly. I turned in a full circle, checking everywhere for a sign of the hairy creatures.

Their low grumbles and growls faded into the distance. The ground stopped shaking.

A gust of cool wind blew through the clearing. It made the gourds in the trees knock against each other. An eerie melody whistled through the trees.

I shuddered.

"Let's get out of here. Now!" Nat cried.

"Wait!" I told him. I grabbed his arm and held him back. "Those beasts are too near. They'll hear us or see us."

"Yeah, well, I'm not going to stick around. I'm going to run as hard as I can. I'm outta here!"

"I'm with you." Pat leaped to his feet. "But which way do we go?" he asked.

"We can't go anywhere now," I argued. "We're lost. We don't know which way to go. So we have to stay right here. Mom and Dad will come find us. I know they will."

"And what if they don't? What if they're in trouble, too?" Nat asked.

"Dad knows how to survive in the woods," I said firmly. "And we don't."

At least I didn't. If only I had listened at that outdoors camp.

"I do, too!" Pat whined. "I can take care of myself. Right Nat? Let's get going!"

Who was he kidding? Pat didn't even *like* the woods.

But he's stubborn. When he gets an idea, no one can change his mind. And Nat always agrees with him. Twins!

"Ginger — are you coming or not?" Pat demanded.

"You're crazy," I told him. "We have to stay here. That's the rule, remember?"

Mom and Dad always told us, if we ever get lost, stay where we are.

"But there are only two of Mom and Dad — and there's three of us," Pat argued. "So we should go find them."

"But they're not the ones who are lost!" I cried.

"I think we should go," Pat repeated. "We have to get away from those ugly creatures!"

"Okay," I told them. "We'll go. At least we'll be together."

I still thought they were wrong. But I couldn't

let them go off without me. What if something horrible happened to them?

Besides, I didn't want to stay in these strange woods alone.

As I turned to follow them, I glimpsed something move in the tall grass.

"It's . . . it's . . . them!" Nat stammered. "They're back!"

I stared at the grass in horror.

"Run!" Pat shrieked. He bolted across the clearing.

A squirrel scurried out of the grass.

"Pat, wait!" Nat yelled.

"It's only a squirrel!" I shouted.

He didn't hear us.

Nat and I took off, chasing after Pat.

"Pat! Hey — Pat!"

I didn't see the thick, twisted root that poked out of the ground. I tripped over it and hit the ground hard. I lay there stunned.

Nat knelt down beside me. He grabbed my arm and helped me to my feet.

I glanced up ahead. Pat had already vanished into the woods. I couldn't see him anywhere.

"We have to catch up to him," I told Nat breathlessly. I straightened up, brushing dirt off my knees.

The earth started to tremble again.

"Oh, no!" Nat moaned.

The creatures were back.

I whirled around. Big blue beasts pushed back through the trees. I counted four behind us. Three on my left. Five to our right.

I gave up counting.

There were too many of them.

The big one grunted and raised its furry paws high in the air. It pointed at us. The other creatures grunted and uttered cries of excitement.

"They've caught us!" I groaned.

"Ginger . . . " Nat whimpered. His eyes opened wide with terror. I clutched at his hand and held it tight.

The beasts drew closer. And formed a circle around us.

Nowhere to run now.

"We're trapped," I whispered.

The beasts began to growl.

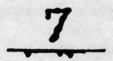

7

Over the drone of their low growls, I heard the eerie melody whistling through the gourds again.

Nat huddled close to me. "They've got us," he whispered. "Do you think — do you think they got Pat?"

I couldn't answer. I couldn't talk.

I felt weak and helpless. Sweat ran down my face into my eyes. I wanted to wipe the sweat away, but I couldn't lift my hand to do it.

I was too scared to move.

Then the beast with the flabby chin stepped forward. It stopped a few inches away from me.

I slowly raised my eyes. I stared at its furry belly. Then its broad chest. I saw shiny, black insects crawling in its fur.

I raised my eyes to its face. Its green eyes glared down at me. It opened its mouth. I stared helplessly at its long fang, chipped on the end.

You don't need a tooth like that for eating *fruit*! I thought.

The beast stretched to its full height. It raised a furry paw high above us. Ready to strike.

Nat huddled closer to me. I could practically feel his heart beating through his T-shirt. Or maybe it was my own heart that was pounding.

The creature growled and swung.

I squeezed my eyes shut.

I felt a slap on my shoulder — so hard it knocked me backwards.

"You're It!" the creature bellowed.

Huh? My mouth dropped open in astonishment.

"You're It," the beast repeated.

I gaped at Nat. His eyes bulged in surprise.

"It . . . it talked!" Nat stammered to me. "In our language."

The creature scowled at Nat. "I talk in many languages," he growled. "We have a universal language adaptor."

"Oh," Nat said weakly. He and I exchanged stunned glances.

The creature growled again and took a step closer to me. "Did you hear me?" he growled. "You're It!"

His marble eyes glared into mine. He tapped a paw impatiently on the ground.

"What do you mean?" I asked.

The creature grunted. "You're the Beast from the East," he said.

"What are you talking about? I'm not a beast. I'm a girl!" I declared. "Ginger Wald."

"I am Fleg," the beast replied, pounding himself on the chest. He waved a paw at the creature beside him, a beast with one eye missing. "This is Spork," Fleg announced. Fleg pounded the other beast on the back.

Spork grunted at Nat and me. I stared at his dark, empty eye socket. And I spotted a deep black scar on the side of Spork's nose.

An eye missing and a scar. The big creature had been in a pretty nasty fight. I hoped it wasn't a fight with a human. Because if Spork was the winner, I would hate to see the loser!

Nat gaped at Spork.

"Uh, this is my brother Nat," I said quickly.

Spork growled in reply.

"Have you seen our mom and dad?" I asked Fleg. "See, we're all here camping, and we got separated. But we're trying to get back together and go home. So, we'd better go — "

"There are others?" Fleg glanced sharply around the clearing. "Where?"

"That's the problem," Nat answered. "We can't find them."

Fleg grunted. "If you can't find them, they can't play."

"Right. That's the rule," Spork agreed. He scratched at the insects that climbed around in his fur.

"Now start moving," Fleg demanded. "It's getting late. And you're It."

I stared at Nat. This was too weird. What did he mean — *they can't play*? And why did he keep saying I was It? Did they want to play tag or something?

The circle of beasts began stomping their paws, shaking the forest ground. "Play . . . play . . . " they chanted.

"Play what?" I demanded. "Is this really some kind of game?"

Spork's eye bulged and a big smile spread under his ugly, pink snout. "The best game," he said. "But you are too slow to win."

Spork rubbed his paws together. He ran his tongue over the tops of his teeth. "You should run." He grunted.

"Yes, run," Fleg ordered. "Before I count to trel."

"Hold on," I protested. "What if we don't want to play?"

"Yeah — why should we?" Nat demanded.

"You have to play," Fleg replied. "Read that sign over there."

He pointed to a cardboard sign tacked to one of the gourd trees. The sign read: GAME IN SEASON.

Fleg stared down at me. His eyes narrowed menacingly. His wet nose flared.

He grinned. Not a friendly grin.

"Game in season?" Nat read the sign in a trembling voice.

31

"You have to tell us how to play," I declared. "I mean, we can't play a game without knowing what it is."

Spork growled deep in his throat and moved closer to me. So close I could smell his fur. What a sour stench!

Fleg reached out a paw and held Spork back.

"It's a good game," Fleg told us. "It's very exciting."

"Uh . . . why is it so exciting?" I asked.

His eyes narrowed. "It's a game of *survival*!" he replied with a grin.

9

Survival?

Oh, no! *No way* I wanted to play!

"You have until the sun sinks behind the Gulla Willow," Fleg declared.

"What's a Gulla Willow?" Nat asked.

"And where is it?" I wanted to know.

"At the edge of the woods," Fleg replied. He waved a paw to the trees.

"Which edge? Where? How will we know which tree?" I demanded.

Fleg flashed Spork a grin. They both made weird choking sounds in their throats.

I could tell they were laughing. All the other creatures started laughing, too. Such an ugly sound. More like gagging than laughing.

"We can't play the game unless we know more," I shouted.

The laughter stopped.

Spork scratched the bugs on his chest. "It's simple. If you're It when the sun goes down, you lose," he told me.

The others grunted in agreement.

"And what happens to the losers?" I asked in a trembling voice.

"We nibble on them," Fleg replied.

"Excuse me?" I asked. "You nibble?"

"Yes, we nibble on them. Until dinnertime. Then we eat them."

10

The creatures around us exploded into more laughter. The sick gagging sound made me feel like puking.

"It's not funny!" Nat shrieked.

Fleg narrowed his eyes at us. "It's our favorite game."

"Well, I don't like your game!" Nat cried.

"We're not going to play. We don't want to," I added.

Spork's eye lit up. "You mean you surrender? You give up?" He smacked his lips hungrily.

"NO!" I shouted. Nat and I jumped back. "We'll play. But by the rules. You have to tell us the rules. All of them."

A cloud rolled overhead. It cast a shadow over the clearing. I shivered.

Were they going to attack us because we didn't want to play?

"Made in the Shade!" Spork cried suddenly.

"Made in the Shade," Fleg repeated.

Huh?

"What's going on?" I demanded.

The cloud slowly passed.

"No time to explain," Fleg said. He waved a paw at the other creatures. "Let's go," he insisted. "This time-out has been too long."

"This isn't fair!" Nat protested. "Please. We need to know the rules."

"Okay," Fleg said as he turned to go. "Gling — you must always attack from the east."

"The east," I mumbled. I raised a hand to shade my eyes as I scanned the clearing.

East. North. South. West. I pictured a map. East was to my right. West to my left. But which direction was east out here in the woods? Why hadn't I listened at that outdoors camp?

"Proo — the brown squares are Free Lunch squares," Fleg continued.

"You mean they're for resting? They're safe?" I asked. I liked that rule. Maybe we could find a brown square and stay there until sunset.

Fleg snorted.

"No. Free Lunch. It means anyone can eat you!" He glared down at me. "Rule Zee," he announced. "You must be three feet tall to play."

I glanced at the beasts. They were at least ten feet tall! So much for Fleg's rules.

"Well, thanks for explaining," I said, shaking my head. "But we really can't play this game. We have to find our parents and — "

36

"You *must* play," Fleg growled. "You're It. You're the Beast from the East. Play — or surrender."

"The sun will be down soon," Spork added, licking his fang.

"You have until the sun goes down behind the Gulla Willow tree," Fleg said. "Then, the Beast from the East is the loser."

Spork made a choking sound, his ugly laugh. "You will make a delicious loser. I'm thinking maybe a sweet-and-sour sauce. Or perhaps you'd go better with something a little more spicy."

The creatures all gagged and choked. They thought Spork was a riot.

Fleg turned to the woods. He stopped. "Oh," he added with an evil grin. "Good luck."

"Good luck," Spork repeated. He poked a finger into his open eye socket and scratched inside it. Then he turned and lumbered after Fleg.

The other creatures followed. The earth trembled under their heavy feet. In a few moments, the clearing stood empty again.

I gaped at Nat.

This wasn't a game! These evil monsters searched the woods for lost kids. And then they —

"What are we going to do?" Nat cried. "Maybe they already ate Pat. Maybe they found him on a brown Free Lunch square."

"And Mom and Dad, too," I murmured.

He let out a frightened gasp.

"There *has* to be someplace safe!" I told him. "The way we use the porch at home when we play tag."

Nat swallowed nervously. "What's safe here?"

I shrugged. "I don't know," I admitted.

"We can call time-out," Nat suggested. "You're always allowed a time-out in every game."

"This is different. This is for our lives," I said softly.

The leaves rustled in the trees above us. The wind made the gourds whistle.

I heard a low growl. Then a creature laughed. That ugly gagging sound. Twigs crackled. Bushes swayed. I heard low grunts.

"We'd better start playing," Nat urged. "They sound hungry."

11

"How can we play?" I cried. "There's no way we can win. There are too many of them. And we don't even know where that Gulla tree is."

"So what?" Nat demanded. "We don't have a choice — do we?"

The leaves in a tree branch over our heads rustled. The branch started thrashing around.

Thud.

I shrieked and leaped back.

Something small and brown hit the ground at my feet.

One of those small, brown animals we had seen earlier. It rubbed up against my leg, and made a gurgling sound.

"At least these little guys aren't mean," Nat said. He reached down to pet it.

The animal snapped at Nat's hand, clamping four rows of tiny, sharp teeth.

"Whooa!" Nat jerked his hand away and leaped

back. The animal scurried into the underbrush.

Nat swallowed hard. "Weird," he murmured. "What kind of forest is this? How come there aren't any *normal* animals?"

"Shhh!" I placed my finger over my lips and scowled. "Listen."

"I don't hear anything," Nat complained.

"Exactly," I answered.

The grunts and growls and choking laughter had vanished. The woods were quiet. *Really* quiet.

"Now's our chance!" I cried. "Let's run for it." I grabbed his hand.

"Wait!" Nat cried. "Which way?"

I squinted around the clearing. "Back to the stream," I declared. "We'll try to follow it back to Mom and Dad. Maybe we'll hear their voices along the water."

"Okay," Nat agreed.

We raced across the clearing. We plunged into the woods and pushed through the thick line of trees.

I peered ahead into the forest. "This way!" I shouted, pointing to my left.

"Why?" Nat asked.

"Because," I said impatiently. "I see light through the trees up ahead. That means the woods thin out. There were fewer trees near the stream, remember?"

I hurried on. Nat followed. We ran silently for a while. The trees did begin to thin out. Soon, scraggly bushes dotted the ground.

"There!" I stopped. Nat nearly crashed into me. "Up ahead."

"The stream!" Nat exclaimed. He slapped me a high five.

Excited now, we began to run. We reached the water at about the same time.

"Now what?" Nat asked.

"Let's head left again," I suggested. "The sun was in our eyes when we started. So now we want it on our backs."

Yes! I thought. We were definitely headed back the way we came. All we had to do now was follow the stream back to the right clearing. Back to our parents.

"Stay low," I told Nat. "Try not to make any noise, just in case." In case the beasts were following us. "And keep an eye out for Pat," I added.

I had no idea if Pat was still in the woods or not. I hoped he had made it back to our camp. But he could be anywhere. Maybe hiding someplace nearby, alone and scared.

Thinking about how scared Pat might be made me feel braver. We had to stay calm so we could help Pat.

Nat and I crouched down. We scooted along the

stream, pushing through the umbrella bushes that grew close to the water's edge.

I could still see the silvery-blue fish circling below the surface of the water.

Gazing at the fish, I stumbled. I grabbed at a leaf on an umbrella bush to steady myself. The leaf shredded in my hand. Blue sap smeared over my fingers.

Not again! Another color. Yellow. Red. And now blue. "Ginger! Come here!"

Nat's cry startled me. I rushed to his side.

Nat pointed to the ground.

I glanced down, afraid of what I would see.

"A footprint," I said, frowning. Then I let out a loud whoop.

Nat's boot rested inside the footprint perfectly. It was exactly the same size as his.

"Pat!" we said together.

"He *has* been here!" Nat cried joyfully.

"Yes!" I shouted. Pat had found his way back to the stream.

"Maybe he already made it back to camp," Nat said excitedly. "We can follow his foot-prints."

We started out eagerly. With each step I pictured Mom and Dad and Pat's smiling faces when Nat and I showed up at camp.

Pat's footprints marched along the stream for a while. Then they veered into the woods.

We followed them through the trees and found

ourselves on a narrow path. The trees grew closer together here.

Overhead, the sun disappeared from view.

The air grew damp and cold.

I heard a familiar growl.

Right behind us.

The ground shook.

"Beasts!" I screamed. "Run!"

I pushed Nat forward. We sprinted down the path. It curved to the right and then back to the left. I had no idea which direction we were going now.

Branches of trees whipped our faces. I struggled to shove them aside. The trees swayed and shook above our heads. Gourds hit the ground all around us.

Something warm and wet tangled itself around my arm. I yanked free. Another wet thing grabbed me.

Vines.

Thick yellow vines.

Some draped over the branches of the trees, dangling onto the forest floor. Others sprouted from the tree trunks. They wrapped around each other, weaving thick nets from tree to tree.

Some vines stretched across the path. Nat and I had to jump and twist, leaping over the vines in our way.

It was hard work. I could hear Nat breathing hard.

My side ached. My breath came in short, sharp bursts.

I longed to rest. But we couldn't rest. The ground was shaking under our feet. The woods echoed with thunderous cries.

The beasts were coming. And they were gaining on us.

"Watch out!" Nat warned.

I spotted a tangled web of vines strung across the path.

Nat jumped the web. He cleared it. I gathered myself and leaped. I jumped high.

But not high enough.

Vines wrapped around my ankles. I fell to the ground.

More thick yellow vines twisted around my legs. Frantically, I grabbed at them and tried to pull them off.

The vines tugged back.

Hard.

"Nat!" I shrieked. "Help!"

"I'm stuck!" he cried. His voice cracked. "Help me, Ginger!"

I couldn't help him. I couldn't move.

I glanced down at my legs. The vines were tugging tighter and tighter.

Another vine inched around my waist.

I gaped down at it.

What were those shiny things?

Eyes?

"Eyes!" I cried out.

Vines don't have eyes!

And then I realized what I was staring at.

The vines weren't vines.

They were snakes.

12

I screamed.

"Ginger!" Nat cried behind me. "These aren't vines. They're — snakes!"

"Tell me something I don't know!" I groaned.

The snake around my waist uncoiled and slithered onto my right arm. It was covered with thick scales that felt rough against my bare skin.

I took a deep breath. Then I wrapped my left hand around the snake's body. It was warm.

I yanked hard. Tried to pull it off.

No way.

The snake coiled tighter around my arm. Its hard, cold eyes stared up at me. Its tongue flicked in and out.

I felt something brush against my thigh. I glanced down.

Another snake climbed up my body.

Sweat ran down my forehead.

"Ginger! Help!" Nat wailed. "They're climbing all over me."

46

"M-me, too!" I stammered. I glanced at my brother. His eyes bulged in terror. He twisted and squirmed, trying to free himself.

The snake around my thigh pulled back its head. And stared at me with those piercing eyes.

The snake around my arm wound tighter and tighter — until my fingers turned numb. It hissed. A long, slow hiss. As if it had all the time in the world.

"They're going to attack!" Nat cried in a strangled voice.

I didn't answer. I felt a wiry tongue flick against my neck.

Cold.

Their tongues were cold.

And prickly.

I squeezed my eyes shut and held my breath.

Don't bite. Please don't bite, I prayed.

A growl disturbed the bushes around us.

"Grrougggh!"

Fleg jumped out of the bushes. He stared at Nat and me, his mouth open.

I gasped.

I saw Fleg's eyes bulge in surprise as he spotted the snakes. "Double Snake Eyes!" he called out.

My entire body trembling, I gaped at him in horror.

Double Snake Eyes?

Was that good — or bad?

13

"Congratulations! Double Snake Eyes!" Fleg cried. He shook his head in wonder. "And you said you never played this game before!"

The snakes tightened around me.

I stared at him. "What are you talking about?" I choked out.

"Twenty points — that's what I'm talking about." The huge beast grunted. "I'd better play harder. Or you're going to win!"

"Who cares about winning!" I screamed. "I can't breathe! Get these snakes off!"

Fleg grinned. "Off!" he screamed with laughter. The folds of skin under his jaw flapped up and down. "That's a good one."

"We mean it," Nat pleaded. "Get them off us!"

Fleg seemed confused. "Why?" He asked. "They might bite you."

"We know!" I screamed. "Help us — please!"

The snakes flicked their tongues against my cheek. My stomach lurched.

Fleg grinned. "If they bite you, you could be awarded a Triple Hisser," he explained. "Worth sixty points."

Points for getting bitten. Some game!

"Forget the points!" I shrieked. "Get — them — off. Now!"

Fleg shrugged. "Okay."

He stepped up to me. Then he pushed a claw under the snake that was coiled around my arm. "You need claws to do this right," he bragged.

Fleg scratched his claw along the snake's skin.

I could feel the snake loosen its grip.

"They're ticklish," Fleg explained. He yanked the snake away and tossed it into the woods.

He tickled the other snake, then pulled it from around my leg. Then he turned to Nat and repeated the same motions, tickling the snakes and prying them loose.

When Fleg was done, he leaped toward the edge of the woods.

I struggled to my feet and rubbed my arms and legs. My whole body itched and tingled. I knew I'd see those snakes in my dreams!

Fleg stuck his furry head out from behind a tree.

"You could have tagged me," he called. "Too bad!"

He opened his mouth in a gagging laugh. Then he plunged into the woods and disappeared.

My mouth dropped open. I stared after him in disbelief.

"Tag!" Nat cried. "Now I get it. It's just like tag. The rules are easy, Ginger." He turned to face me. "Touch one of the beasts, and you won't be It anymore. You won't be the Beast from the East!"

Nat took off, running after Fleg.

"Wait, Nat!" I started after him. I stepped on something hard. I heard a crunch.

Another crunch. I glanced down.

"Nat! Stop!" I screamed. I spotted an orange rock at my feet. I picked it up and hurled it after Nat. "Hey — stop!"

I glanced down at my hand. Orange. My fingers had turned orange where they had grasped the rock.

The rock smacked into a tree trunk. Nat stopped. Whirled around. "What did you do that for?" he cried.

"To stop you," I answered.

"Listen, Ginger," Nat urged. "You have to tag one of the beasts. It's the only way to win the game. To stay alive."

"I don't think so," I said as calmly as I could.

Nat scowled. "What's your problem? It's just like tag."

"No," I said. "This is *not* just like tag. Not the game that we used to play."

I pointed at the ground.

Nat stepped closer. He gazed down to where I was pointing.

He gasped. "What *is* that?" he asked.

14

"Bones," I murmured. "A pile of animal bones."

Nat and I stared. The bones gleamed coldly in the sunlight. Picked clean.

"Notice anything else?" I pointed to the ground beside the bones.

"What?" Nat frowned.

"It's brown," I said. "The grass under the bones. It's a square brown patch."

Free Lunch.

Nat swallowed hard.

"A beast ate it," he murmured. "Whatever it was."

I wrapped my arms around my chest. "This is not like tag, Nat," I told him solemnly. I couldn't take my eyes off the poor animal's bones. "This game is deadly."

"Only if we lose," Nat said. "Ginger, we just saw Fleg. He helped us."

"So?" I asked.

"So, we'll make him help us again."

"How can we do that?"

Nat grinned. "Easy. We'll trick him. Pretend to need help. Pretend you have another snake on you or something."

"Right," I replied, rolling my eyes. Like I was really going to let Fleg near me again.

Nat grabbed my arm. "It'll work. You scream for help. Fleg gets close. You jump out and tag him. Easy." Nat snapped his fingers.

I shook my head. "Forget it. I'm going to find the stream again and get out of here."

"Why are you so stubborn?" Nat cried.

"Because I'm It!" I screamed. "I'm the one they're going to eat!"

"I-I know we can win if we try," Nat stammered.

I took a few deep breaths and tried to get rid of the panic in my chest.

"Okay," I said finally. "Okay. Okay. I'll try it. What should I do?"

15

Nat beamed at me. "First I'll climb a tree," he said. "I can spot the beasts' hiding places from up there."

I gazed up at the tall, leafy trees around us.

I thought about it. All we needed was to tag one beast. Any beast.

"Do it," I told Nat. "But don't stay up there too long."

Nat searched the woods for the best tree. "That one," he said finally.

The tree was tall. Dozens of sturdy branches sprang from its sides. In the center of each branch was a big, strong knot. Tiny golden leaves covered the branches. The tree looked strong, strong enough to hold Nat.

"This is a cinch," he assured me. "As easy as climbing a ladder. I'll be able to see *everything* from up there."

I waited near the base of the tree.

Nat placed his foot on the lowest branch and hoisted himself up.

He climbed slowly. Steadily.

"See anything yet?" I called anxiously.

"I see a weird nest," he shouted down. "With big eggs."

"What about the beasts?" I yelled. "Do you see them?"

"Not yet." Nat climbed higher. A few seconds later, he disappeared from view.

"Nat! Can you hear me?" I called. I cupped my hands around my mouth. "Nat! Where are you? Answer me!"

I rushed around the tree, peering up through the branches. I spotted Nat near the very top.

Nat was moving carefully. He let go of one branch and pulled himself onto the next highest branch. The top of the tree swayed dangerously.

I caught my breath.

Maybe this wasn't such a good idea.

Not if I had to climb up and rescue him.

"Nat!" My throat hurt from shouting so loud. "Be careful!"

The trunk swayed back and forth. Slowly at first. Then faster.

Bits of loose bark broke off and fell in slow spirals toward the ground.

The thick branches swished back and forth. Each branch started to bend in the middle.

At the knots.

I stared. The branches reminded me of some-thing. Something familiar.

Arms, I thought. The knots were like elbows. And the branches were like big arms, reach-ing . . .

I blinked. Was I seeing things?

The branches *were* reaching.

They were reaching for Nat.

"Nat!" I screamed.

High above me, I saw him grasp onto a slender branch.

"Nat!" I ran frantically around the base of the tree, pounding my fists on the trunk. "Nat! Come down!" I yelled. "The tree is alive!"

16

Nat peered down at me from the top of the tree. "What's wrong?" he called down.

"Come down!" I screamed. "The branches — "
I was too late.

The upper branches grabbed at Nat's arms. Pinned them to his side. I saw him gasp in shock.

Other branches lashed out, slapping at him.

Slapping him. Whipping him.

"Ginger!" Nat screamed. "Help me!"

What could I do?

I gazed up in horror as two lower branches reached up toward Nat. The top branches passed him down to the lower branches.

The branches wrapped around him, hugging tight.

This isn't happening! I told myself. This *can't* be happening!

Nat's feet dangled in the air. He kicked furiously at the tree. "Let me go! Let me gooooo!"

More branches lashed out. Some held him tight. Others swiped at him, slapping at him.

The branches passed Nat down.

They were carrying him lower, down to the center of the tree.

Where the branches were the thickest.

Where the tree's arms were strongest.

Nat cried out. He kicked out again and again. The branches wrapped around his legs.

No way to climb up to him. Every branch was thrashing wildly. Even the little thin ones that couldn't reach Nat were clawing upwards. Straining to take a swipe at him.

As I watched helplessly, the thickest branches pulled Nat into the center.

He disappeared.

"Help!" His muffled cry drifted down to me. "Ginger — it's going to *swallow* me!"

I had to do something. Had to pull him away somehow. Had to free him from the living tree.

But how?

We had gotten rid of the snakes. We had to get rid of the branches, too. If only . . .

That's it!

I had a crazy idea. But maybe, just maybe it would work.

If the tree is alive, maybe it has feelings, I thought.

And if it has feelings, maybe it's ticklish — just as the snakes were!

"Ginger! Help!" Nat's cries grew weaker.

I knew I didn't have much time.

I leaped at the tree. A branch dipped down and slapped at me.

I jumped back and scrambled around the trunk. I ducked as a thick branch swung at me.

The tree was trying to keep me away while it swallowed up my brother. But I ducked beneath the slapping limbs and branches.

Reached out. And began to tickle the rough bark.

Tickled it with one hand. Then with both.

Was that a shiver? Did the tree actually shiver?

Or did I imagine it?

Please! I silently begged. Please, please, let go of my brother.

I tickled furiously with both hands. "Nat!" I called. "Nat! Can you hear me?"

Silence.

"Nat? Nat?"

No answer.

17

I didn't give up. I tickled harder.

The trunk started to jiggle.

Bunches of leaves shook free and floated down. They landed in my hair and covered my arms as I jabbed and scratched at the tree trunk.

I tickled harder. The branches shook and swayed. The trunk wriggled.

Yes! I thought excitedly. It's working! I think it *is* ticklish!

I'll make this tree collapse with laughter!

I tickled harder. The trunk squirmed under my fingertips.

I glanced up. Nat's boots poked through the leaves.

Then his legs. His arms. His face.

The branches were shaking. Quivering and shaking.

Nat swung free. He leaped from branch to branch. His tree-climbing skills were finally coming in handy!

"Hurry!" I shouted up to him. "I can't keep this up much longer. Jump!"

Nat wriggled down the tree trunk.

"Here goes!" Nat cried. He let go of the trunk and leaped into the air.

He landed in a crouched position at my feet. "Whoa! Good job, Ginger!"

I grabbed his hand and we hurtled away from the tree.

Nat brushed twigs and leaves from his hair. "I saw some beasts!"

I bit my lip. In all the excitement over the living tree, I had forgotten we were playing a deadly game.

"I saw three of them," Nat reported. "Fleg, Spork, and another one with a smashed tail. That way." He pointed to the right.

"What were they doing?" I asked.

"They are all hiding behind a big, gray boulder. You can sneak up on them, easy."

"Right." I rolled my eyes. "Piece of cake."

"You can do it." Nat's dark eyes locked on mine. "I know you can, Ginger."

Nat led the way. We crept slowly through the woods toward the boulder.

The sky dimmed overhead and the air grew cooler. I knew that it was nearly evening. Soon the sun would disappear behind the Gulla Willow tree.

I hoped I had enough time.

"There's the rock!" Nat whispered.

I saw a small clearing in the trees. In the middle of the clearing a craggy, gray boulder rose up from the flat ground.

It was big enough to hide a dozen beasts.

My heartbeat quickened.

"I'll hide behind this cabbage plant," Nat said.

He ducked behind the plant. I followed. I wasn't quite ready to face the beasts alone.

I bent down and tightened my bootlace, trying to ignore the fluttering in my stomach.

"Just sneak up on them," Nat whispered.

"Come with me," I begged.

Nat shook his head. "Too noisy if we both go," he said. "It's safer if you go alone."

I knew he was right.

Besides, I told myself, it was pretty easy. The beasts behind the big rock had no idea I was coming. All I had to do was tag one of them.

I felt a thrill of excitement. I could do it.

And the game would be over. We'd be safe.

I took a deep breath. "Ready or not, here I come," I whispered.

I crept toward the boulder. I glanced back. Nat poked his head from behind the cabbage and flashed me a thumbs-up sign.

A few more steps and I'd be at the rock. I held my breath.

The gray rock rose up in front of me.

I reached out. My fingers were trembling with excitement.

I leaped behind the rock.

"Gotcha," I cried. "You're It!"

18

"Huh?"

My hand swiped empty air.

They were gone!

No beasts. Only a pile of broken gourds scattered over the ground.

I blinked in surprise. And scrambled to the front of the rock.

No beasts. They had moved on.

"Nat!" I called. "Nat!"

My brother came jogging to the boulder. "What happened?"

"Nothing happened. They're gone," I told him. "Now what?"

"Hey," Nat snapped. "It's not *my* fault."

I stared at him, feeling totally disappointed. And afraid.

A sharp gust of wind kicked up. I glanced at the sky. Shades of pink streaked overhead. The sun was setting.

My chest tightened in despair.

"It's hopeless," I muttered.

Nat shook his head. "Do you know what we need?" he asked.

"No. What?" I replied.

"We need another plan."

I had to laugh. Nat was such a jerk!

He leaned against the boulder and wrinkled his nose. "What kind of rock is this anyway?" he asked.

"A creepy one," I answered.

Nat peered at the huge rock. "Something's growing on it," he said.

"Well, don't touch anything," I warned.

But telling Nat not to do something only makes him want to do it more.

Nat stuck his finger into a hole in the boulder.

The big rock trembled.

A crack appeared at its top and spread quickly.

Nat pulled his finger away.

"What's happening?" I yelled.

A cloud of gray smoke shot up from inside the boulder.

KERPLOOM!

Nat and I ducked, clapping our hands over our ears.

The explosion roared like a million firecrackers going off at once.

More gray smoke billowed out of the boulder.

I could barely see Nat. I started to cough. My eyes burned.

The smoke filled the clearing around us and drifted above the treetops. A few seconds later, it faded away.

And I saw Fleg standing in the clearing.

Spork appeared behind him, scratching at his open eye socket.

Another beast followed. And then another. They stared at Nat and me.

"You touched the Penalty Rock!" Fleg cried.

Nat took a step closer to me. "Huh?"

Fleg nodded to the beast with the smashed tail. "Get him, Gleeb," Fleg growled.

Gleeb's snout tensed. His eyes bulged. He reached out for Nat's arm.

"Wait! Stop," I yelled. "Nat didn't know it was a penalty."

"No fair! No fair!" Nat cried.

The beasts ignored us.

Gleeb scooped Nat up and lifted him high in the air. "Let's go," Gleeb grunted.

Gleeb balanced Nat on both paws. Then he pretended to drop him.

Nat shrieked.

Gleeb and the other beasts snorted their ugly laughter, clapping their hairy paws together.

"Stop it!" I screamed. "Let him go!"

"Yes, go," the beasts echoed. They clapped their paws again. "Let's go! Let's go!" they chanted.

I glared at Fleg. "Tell him to put my brother down."

"He touched the Penalty Rock," Fleg explained. "He must have his penalty."

"But we didn't know about it!" I protested. "We don't know any of your dumb rules. That isn't fair."

I tried to grab Nat's dangling legs.

"Let me see your hand," Fleg demanded. He snatched at my arm and lifted my hand up to his eyes. He studied my palm.

"Nubloff colors!" he exclaimed. He studied me. "That's fifty points. You can't trick me. You've played this game before. You already know the rules."

I stared at my hand. Yellow sap from the stick. Blue from the leaf of the umbrella plant. Orange from the rock. Nubloff colors?

"But . . . but . . . " I stammered. "I didn't get these colors on purpose. They just happened."

Fleg and Spork exchanged glances.

"Come," Fleg ordered, waving to Gleeb.

Gleeb tossed Nat over his shoulder and followed Fleg to the woods. The others stomped after them.

"Ginger!" Nat wailed as the beast carried him away.

I ran after them, feeling totally helpless.

"Stop! Where are you taking him?" I shrieked. "What are you going to do to him?"

19

I chased after them. Down a wide path lined with more giant rocks.

More penalty boulders?

I stayed in the center of the path, afraid to touch them.

The beasts stopped at the entrance to a tunnel. It was carved into the side of the largest rock I had seen. They ducked their heads and hurried inside.

I followed behind, my heart pounding.

"Ginger!" Nat's cry echoed off the tunnel walls.

The beasts growled and grunted, jabbering in excitement. Some pounded their paws on the ceiling as they moved.

Everything shook. The walls. The ceiling. The ground.

"Nat!" I cried. I couldn't hear my own voice over the noise.

I followed the beasts out of the tunnel and into another large clearing.

"What's *that*?" I gasped.

In the center of the clearing, a large wooden box hung from a tree. It looked like an enormous bird house. I saw a tiny door on one side.

A sign above the door read: PENALTY CAGE.

Gleeb raised Nat high in the air. He held him up for all the beasts to see and spun him around and around.

Nat screamed.

Spork and the other beasts stomped and clapped.

"NO!" I shouted. "You can't do this!"

"He must go in the box," Fleg declared. "He touched the Penalty Rock. It's in the rules."

Gleeb tossed Nat inside the Penalty Cage. He slammed the door. Fleg dropped a large twig into the rough wooden latch to lock the door.

Nat reached through the slats. "Ginger," he cried. "Get me out of here." The penalty box swung in the air.

"Don't worry, Nat," I called. "I'll get you out." I shivered. He seemed so small and helpless.

"You can't keep him in there forever," I told Fleg. "When does he get out?"

"When we eat him," Fleg replied softly.

20

"But I'm the Beast from the East!" I protested. "You said you would eat *me*." I took a step closer to him.

"Players in the Penalty Cage get eaten, too." Fleg snorted in disgust. "Don't pretend you forgot. Everyone knows that. It's a basic rule."

"There must be another way to get him out," I said, edging closer.

"Only if he eats a Free Escape Tarantula," Fleg explained. He scratched the flab under his chin.

"Huh? He has to eat a tarantula?" I demanded, taking another step toward the beast.

Fleg narrowed his eyes. "Don't pretend you don't know *that*," he said, beginning to turn away.

I hurled myself at Fleg's hairy chest.

I slapped him hard.

"You're It!" I screamed. I lifted both fists in triumph. "You're It! I tagged you!"

Fleg raised an eyebrow. "Sorry," he said calmly. "I paused the game. It doesn't count."

"No!" I shrieked. "You can't! You can't keep changing the rules!"

"I didn't. Rules are rules." Fleg reached over me and checked the lock on Nat's cage. It held fast.

"Try again," Spork grunted. "You can always try again."

The rest of the beasts nodded in agreement, grinning and snorting in excitement. They were enjoying themselves. They rumbled away from the clearing.

"Ginger!" Nat cried. He pounded on the box. "Get me out of here!"

I gazed at him in despair. No way could I reach him up there.

He stared down at me through the slats. His brown hair fell into his eyes. "Do something," he pleaded.

"I'll try again," I said.

It was the only thing to do.

"Can you see them?" I called up to him. "Which way did they go?"

Nat pointed. "I see a few beasts hiding over there."

"I'll be back," I promised. "After I tag one of them."

I tried to sound as if it was a sure thing. I wished I could believe my own words.

"Hurry!" Nat called after me.

A strong wind blew through the clearing, rocking the cage from side to side. Nat hunched down, hugging his knees.

I gave him one last look and took off.

Long shadows fell across the ground. I gazed at the sky. The orange was turning into deep pink. Almost sundown.

I plunged into the darkening woods.

All around me I could hear small animals skittering through the carpet of leaves on the forest floor. As if hurrying home before sunset.

Home. Where they were safe.

The wind howled loudly through the trees. I stumbled and almost fell over a rotted tree stump.

The woods were closing in on me. Time was closing in on me.

And then I saw a beast hiding behind an umbrella bush. His shoulders slumped forward. His head bobbed gently up and down.

He was sound asleep.

Here's my chance, I thought.

I moved slowly toward him. The beast shifted position.

I stopped. Held my breath.

He quieted down again. He must have moved in his sleep.

This is it, I thought. My chance. In a second, he'll be the Beast from the East.

I rushed forward.

And gasped.

The earth dropped away.
Nothing under me.
Nothing but air.
I fell quickly. Sank straight down.
Down . . . down . . . down . . .
Screaming all the way.

21

I hit solid ground.

Hard.

The air burst from my lungs.

My shoulder jammed against a sharp rock.

I cried out. Rubbed my arm.

Struggling to catch my breath, I pulled myself up and stared around me.

Too dark. I couldn't see a thing.

It's over, I thought. The game is over.

"Hey — is anyone up there?" I called. "Can anyone hear me?"

I stopped and listened for an answer. Any answer.

Silence.

I forced myself to my feet. My shoulder ached. I rolled it back and forth a couple of times to keep it from getting stiff.

I reached out and patted the walls around me. Solid dirt. I was in some sort of deep pit. The kind people dig to trap animals.

Now I was the trapped animal.

I ran my hands quickly over the walls. Maybe I could find something to hold onto. Some way to climb out.

Yuck! What was that?

My hand touched something cold sticking out of the side of the pit.

I clenched my teeth and forced myself to touch it again. It stayed firm under my fingers. A root, I thought excitedly.

It's not alive.

I ran my hand further up the wall. The roots were everywhere. As high up as I could feel. Perfect!

I raised my foot and stepped onto the lowest root. It held.

Footholds! I could climb out of the pit.

My hands grabbed the highest root I could reach. I pulled myself up. I heard a crumbling of loose dirt.

I pressed myself against the wall as more dirt sifted down the side of the pit, spraying my face.

I squeezed my eyes shut. Waited for the dirt to stop falling. Then I found the next root and began climbing again.

How much time did I have left? How much time before the sun went down?

My shoulder ached. But I had a long way to go. I rested briefly against the wall. Then I continued climbing.

Snap!

The root shattered under my right foot. My leg dangled in the air.

Snap!

The root under my right hand popped loose.

"Hey!" I cried out as I felt myself fall.

I landed hard on the floor of the pit. I lay still for a moment, trying to catch my breath.

I gazed up. A last bit of pink sky glowed over the mouth of the pit.

In the fading light, I looked around. I saw the useless roots on the sides of the deep hole. I glanced down.

Oh, no.

There was just enough sunlight to see the ground beneath me.

It was brown.

And square.

A Free Lunch square.

I was trapped. Trapped on a Free Lunch square. The beasts could eat me — anytime they wanted.

I froze in panic. And heard rumbling footsteps above me.

I huddled in a corner of the pit. Pressed my back against the dirt.

"This way!" I heard Fleg shout. "She's down here!"

22

Fleg appeared in the opening above me. His flabby chin hung down. His eyes locked onto mine.

"Found you!" he cried.

Spork slid next to Fleg. He grinned down at me and drooled yellow drool. It splattered beside my boot.

"Something down there smells delicious!" Spork cried. "I'm soooo hungry!"

Gleeb shoved his furry face between Fleg's and Spork's.

He smacked his lips. I heard his stomach growl.

"Finally!" Spork grunted. "Pull her out! Let's eat!"

I covered my face with my hands. "Please. Don't hurt me," I cried. "I haven't done anything to you."

Fleg shrugged. "You play the game. Sometimes you win. Sometimes you lose."

Spork and Gleeb reached down into the pit. Their big paws swiped at me.

I pressed my back tighter against the wall. "Please," I begged. "Please go away and leave me alone. You win, okay? You can have all my points."

"Points can't be given away," Fleg scolded. "You know that."

The others grunted in agreement. They reached down for me.

My eyes searched the pit.

I needed a weapon.

The roots?

I yanked a fat one out of the dirt.

"Stay back!" I shouted, whipping the root at their paws.

The beasts slapped each other on the back and laughed their ugly laugh.

"You'll be sorry," I threatened.

Who was I kidding? This stupid root couldn't hurt them. And they knew it. I was the Beast from the East. I was dinner.

Fleg leaned into the pit and snarled. His claws were only inches from my face.

I ducked.

His paw brushed against the back of my neck. I felt claws scratch my skin.

I jerked away. The hair on my arms stood straight up.

If only I could burrow into the earth like an animal, I thought.

Fleg's paw swiped the air in front of my face.

"Stop ducking away," he shouted. "You're just making me hungrier."

"This isn't fair!" I screamed.

He turned to Spork and Gleeb. "I'm tired of this," he complained. "Enough stalling."

His round eyes gleamed down hungrily at me. "Get her!" he bellowed.

Spork leaned down and grabbed my arm. I felt his claws dig into my skin. He pulled me up and yanked me to my feet.

It's all over, I thought sadly. The game is over.

23

A cloud passed overhead, throwing the pit into deep shadow.

Fleg howled. He slapped his broad forehead. "Made in the Shade!" he cried.

Spork opened his paw and let go of my arm.

I dropped to the ground. Fell to my knees.

"Made in the Shade!" Spork cried.

"Made in the Shade!" Gleeb echoed.

I climbed to my feet. The angry voices of the beasts made my head throb.

They stomped their feet loudly.

"What's going on?" I demanded.

"You're safe," Spork replied, sneering in disgust. "This time."

Safe? I breathed a sigh of relief.

"But . . . why?" I asked, amazed.

"You're Made in the Shade," Fleg explained.

"We can't touch you. It's a free pass. But you can only use it once."

Once was enough, I hoped. I didn't plan to play this game forever.

"We have to let you go this time," Fleg growled. "But you're still the Beast from the East."

"You still have to tag someone before sundown," Spork agreed.

Gleeb sighed. The three beasts turned to the woods. "We'll go now," Fleg announced.

"Wait!" I scrambled to my feet. "How do I get out of here? How can I tag someone if I'm stuck in this pit?"

Fleg rolled his eyes. He reached down and pressed one paw against a purple rock on the ground near the edge of the pit.

The pit floor creaked and groaned.

Then it rose up. Higher and higher.

Finally it jerked to a halt a few feet below the ground.

I was close enough to stare at the beasts' ankles. I could see shiny black bugs crawling in their fur. I swallowed nervously. Was this some kind of trick? Or was I really safe?

"I still need help to climb out of here," I told Fleg.

Fleg pounded on the purple rock again.

The floor started moving. This time it stopped level with the ground.

I hopped off the Free Lunch square. The beasts circled me.

"The sun is almost down," Fleg warned. "The game is almost over."

"You don't have much time," Spork added.

Fleg snorted. Then he turned and lumbered away.

"Good luck," Spork cried as he hurried after Fleg. Gleeb followed. They raced back toward the stone tunnel.

"Wait!" I yelled. I ran after them as fast as I could.

I raced into the rock tunnel. I could hear the beasts up ahead of me. They growled and grunted, scraping their claws across the walls and ceiling again. Making a racket.

I saw them burst through the other side of the tunnel. They split up, running in different directions.

Which way should I go? I knew I couldn't waste time.

I followed Fleg.

He wove in and out between the trees. He leaped over some scraggly bushes.

I panted, straining to keep up.

Fleg picked up the pace.

Faster and faster.

I could barely keep up now. I was gasping for air.

"Wait!" I shouted desperately. "Wait!"

Fleg glanced once over his shoulder. He disappeared into the trees. I stopped running after him.

Overhead, the sky turned to purple. Soon it would be completely dark.

I spun around, searching desperately for a beast to tag.

"Yoo-hoo! Over here!" I heard a call.

I whirled around.

Spork. He waved to me from between two tall trees.

I raced toward him.

Spork lumbered down a twisting path. I followed him.

What else could I do?

Suddenly, my foot caught on a rock. I sprawled into the dirt.

I forced myself to get up. The woods were quiet around me.

No beasts.

I wanted to scream! So I did.

"Fleg! Spork! Gleeb! Where are you?" I shouted. How could I tag them? I couldn't even find them.

My eyes scanned the area.

What was that? I squinted harder.

Yes! A blue furry head! It popped up behind a bush.

My last chance.

I gathered my energy and sprinted toward the bush.

My hand reached out.

"Tag!" I yelled. "You're — "

24

"*Gurraugh!*" The tiny beast pawed the air.

The baby beast! The only beast under three feet tall. Too short to play the game.

No fair! I thought.

My hopes were crushed. Again.

I picked up a rock and heaved it angrily into the woods.

"Where is everyone?" I screamed. "Come out and play!"

The little beast patted its claws together and gurgled happily.

I stared at it. Why was it here all alone?

Then it hit me. Of course.

There must be another beast nearby. A grown-up beast to watch the kid. One over three feet tall.

One I could tag.

I checked out the area. Trees and large rocks. I would have to search behind every one of them.

Taking a deep breath, I tiptoed silently through the trees. Stopped to peer behind each rock.

Crunch. My foot cracked a pile of twigs.

I stood completely still. And waited.

Silence.

I moved forward.

I listened carefully.

Silence.

I crept forward. A beast had to be here somewhere.

But where?

Then I heard a noise.

Mumbling.

I crept behind a bush and inched closer to the sound. It came from behind a tall, jagged rock.

I peeked out.

Spork!

Yes! Spork stood behind the rock, talking to himself. He scratched the lumpy scar on his nose.

I could easily tag him.

But was this another penalty rock?

Would it go up in smoke?

I didn't want to end up in a cage dangling above the ground.

Like Nat. Poor Nat.

I took another deep breath and inched closer to Spork.

Spork turned and searched the woods behind

him. "Little beast," he called out. "Is that you?"

I dropped to the ground and waited.

My heart pounded in my ears. I forced myself to stay quiet.

Spork didn't move from his spot. He sighed and started mumbling again.

Three more steps and I could tag him.

Two more.

I wiped my forehead. One more.

It was too good to be true. Spork had no idea I was behind him.

I smacked him hard. "You're It!" I shrieked.

Spork gasped in surprise. His big paws shot up into the air. I thought he was about to faint!

"I've done it! I've done it!" I cried happily.

I was free!

Nat was free!

Spork grunted and raised himself up. He towered over me. He didn't seem the least bit upset. But he had just lost the game.

"You're It!" I repeated. "You're the Beast from the East!"

Spork raised a paw lazily and scratched his open eye socket.

I felt a chill of fear. What if Spork refused to obey the rules?

"Sorry," Spork said softly. "Not this time."

"Hey — !" I shouted angrily. "You have to obey the rules! I tagged you, fair and square!"

Spork stared at me as if I were being very funny.

Something was wrong.

But what? What was it?

Why didn't he say something?

Spork's lips curled into a nasty grin.

25

"You tagged me from the west," Spork whispered. "It doesn't count."

I could feel the blood rush to my face. "No fair! I tagged you! I tagged you!" I wailed.

Spork shrugged.

"You have to tag me from the east. Remember?" Spork's little eyes nearly disappeared as his face crumpled in laughter. "You're *still* the Beast from the East!"

I groaned.

How could I have forgotten? That was the most important rule of all.

How was I supposed to know which way was east? I couldn't even see the sun anymore!

My head throbbed. My whole body ached. I was sore and hungry.

Spork stood there, shaking with silent laughter.

I glanced at the darkening sky.

Wait a minute!

I climbed up on the boulder. The sun was setting

behind me. That was the west. In front of me was east.

I studied Spork. Without Fleg around, the big beast seemed less menacing. Harmless almost.

After all, he was supposed to be baby-sitting. And what had happened? He'd lost the little beast.

And now he was so busy laughing at my mistake, he had practically forgotten about me.

"Hey, Spork," I called. "Do you want to play one of *my* games now?"

"But we're still playing this one." Spork blinked in surprise.

"I'll pause it. It's kind of boring anyway, isn't it?" I asked. "My game is lots more fun."

Spork scratched the hole where his eye used to be. He pulled a big, black bug out of it, and tossed the bug away. "What's your game called?"

"Freeze Frame," I answered quickly.

Nat and Pat loved to play this game.

"We spin around and when I say stop, we freeze — and see if one of us can keep our balance and not fall over."

"Sounds fun," Spork agreed. "Why not?"

"Okay then," I said. "Let's try it. Spin!" I shouted.

We both started to spin.

I peeked at Spork. His arms swung out as he whirled around.

"Faster!" I called out. "Much faster."

Spork whirled faster and faster as he turned around in circles.

His tail swished against the bushes. I jumped out of the way.

Spork started to wobble.

"Game — *unpaused*!" I shouted.

Spork didn't seem to hear me. He teetered and stumbled into a tree.

"Freeze!" I shouted.

Spork froze in place.

I leaped at him and tagged him. Hard.

From the east.

"You're It!" I shouted. I backed away. "I tagged you from the east! This time you're really It!"

Spork placed both paws against his head and closed his eyes. I could tell he was still dizzy. He spread his legs and balanced himself against the tree.

He bopped himself in the face with his paw. "You did it," he agreed. He ran his bumpy tongue over his lips. He exhaled a deep breath. "I'm It," he admitted.

"Yes. Yes. Yes!" I cried. I jumped up in excitement.

Spork plopped down against the boulder.

"I'm free!" I shrieked. "The game is over." I clenched my hand into a fist and pumped my arm.

"I'm going to rescue Nat," I said. "Which way is he?"

Spork pointed his clawed finger to my right.

"We're outta here!" I shouted.

I'd never been so happy in all my life.

"Well, Spork old pal," I said, beaming at him. "This is good-bye. See you!"

"Not so quick," Spork said. "I'm afraid you can't leave."

26

"Forget it," I said. "You can't change the rules again! No way."

"You can't leave," he repeated. "The game continues until sunset." He glared at me stubbornly.

I gazed at the sky. The purple was fading to gray. Not much time left. But enough.

I wasn't going to be It again.

I could hide until dark. But where?

"Don't just stand there," Spork warned. "You could be tagged again."

"Never," I insisted. "I won't let that happen."

Before I could move, Fleg stomped from behind a tree. The flabby skin under his chin swung from side to side.

Gleeb crept behind him.

"She tagged me!" Spork told them.

"I knew it!" Fleg stared at me. "I knew you played this game before."

I balled my hands into fists. I was angry. I'd had enough.

They forced me to play their stupid game. But I wasn't going to lose now.

Fleg waved me away. "You have until I count to trel," he said. "Then we're allowed to come after you again."

He turned his back and covered his eyes. "Gling . . . proo . . . zee . . . freen . . . trel," he counted.

I had no choice. I ran.

Don't stop, I told myself. Don't think about anything. Run. Find a place to hide.

"Ready or not — here we come!" I heard Fleg cry.

Behind me, the beasts growled and grunted in excitement.

I hurled myself off the path and pushed through the tall, scratchy grass between the trees. I jumped over a clump of cabbage plants.

My legs ached. My feet burned.

But I couldn't stop.

Not until I reached a hiding place.

I skidded to a stop when I heard rushing water. I nearly fell into the stream. A large blue fish leaped out of the water and snapped at my ankles.

This was no place to hide. I turned back into the woods.

A cold wind blew in my face. The gourds whistled their strange melody.

"Here I come!" Spork shouted off to my left.

I pushed myself faster. No way he was going to tag me.

I glanced around. Which way?

The rock tunnel! I saw it only a few feet away.

I darted into the darkness. Without the beasts yelling and shouting, it was eerily quiet inside. I slowed down and tiptoed through the tunnel.

When I reached the other side, I crept into the dense trees. I slumped against a tree and waited, trying to keep quiet. I was breathing so hard I was afraid the beasts could hear me!

A moment passed.

I felt the trembling that meant the beasts were approaching.

I held my breath and ducked beneath an umbrella plant.

Seconds later, Fleg, Spork, and Gleeb burst out of the tunnel and raced down the path. Four more beasts followed behind them. They passed the bush where I hid. Crashed into the woods. And kept going.

I waited to make sure they were gone.

Silence.

I breathed a sigh of relief.

I scrambled to my feet and stretched.

Something rushed at me from behind.

"No!" I cried in terror.

Two arms wrapped around my waist. And a creature threw me to the ground.

27

I thrashed and kicked wildly.

"Stop it. Cut it out!" a familiar voice demanded.

"Nat!" I screamed. I whirled around. "Nat! You're safe! How did you get out of the cage?"

"Cage? What cage?" My brother squinted at me.

"The penalty cage," I declared. "Nat — how did you escape? Did they let you go?"

"I'm not Nat. It's me. Pat."

"Pat?" I stared at him in confusion. Then I threw my arms around his neck. I'd never been so happy to see him.

"Where have you been?" I demanded.

"Where have *I* been?" Pat cried. "Where have *you* been? I've been searching everywhere for you guys. These woods are creepy."

He glanced around. "Where's Nat, anyway?"

"Trapped." I started to explain. "See, the beasts got him. After you ran into the woods, we had to play this game and . . ."

"A game?" Pat cried. He shook his head in disbelief. "I was lost in the woods — and you two are playing a game?"

"It's not what you think," I said.

I checked the trees around us for any sign of the creatures.

"They forced us to play," I told Pat, lowering my voice to a whisper. "It's like tag — only they play for keeps. I was the Beast from the East and — "

"Right." Pat rolled his eyes.

"Really," I insisted. "This game is deadly. You have to believe me."

"Why?" Pat shrugged. "You never believe me. Why should I believe you?"

"Because if we lose, they'll *eat* us!" I told him.

Pat burst out laughing.

"I'm serious!" I grabbed Pat's shoulders and shook him hard. "I'm telling the truth! It's dangerous here. Fleg and Spork are after me, right now."

Pat twisted out of my grasp. "Right. Fleg and Spork. Woof woof!" Pat barked.

"Shhh," I hissed. "Keep quiet!" I pulled him behind an umbrella plant. "Pat, you have to believe me. They're all around us. They could get us if we're not careful."

"And I suppose this game was their idea?" he asked.

"Yes," I answered.

"And I suppose they can talk," Pat went on. "In English."

"Yes. Yes. Yes," I insisted.

"You're weirder than I thought," Pat said, shaking his head. "So where's Nat? For real?"

"*Grrraugh!*"

A deep growl echoed off the nearby rocks. "This way!" A beast bellowed. "Near the tunnel!"

Heavy footsteps pounded closer. The ground shook under our feet.

Pat's eyes widened in shock. He reached for my arm.

"It's them!" I exclaimed. "*Now* do you believe me?"

Pat swallowed hard and nodded his head. "Yes. I believe you," he choked out.

"She's over here!" a beast shouted.

"He heard us," I whispered in Pat's ear. "Run!"

Pat and I took off.

We raced through the woods, leaping over fallen logs, pushing sharp branches out of our faces.

"This way!" I called. I grabbed Pat's hand. "Stay low."

We ducked into a thick clump of trees.

Spork thudded past us.

I could hear him sniffing the air.

"Can he smell us?" Pat asked in a whisper.

"Sshh!" I pressed my finger to my lips.

We crept between the bushy plants.

Fleg appeared, stomping in our direction.

I dropped to my hands and knees. I pulled Pat down beside me.

Fleg thudded past us.

I knew we weren't safe. More beasts would follow. And one of them might find us.

I motioned for Pat to follow me.

We scrambled deeper into the woods.

The trees were close together here. The bushes were so thick I couldn't see between them. I flung out an arm, feeling my way.

My hand brushed against something.

Something big.

And warm.

And furry.

28

I leaped back. Crashed into Pat.

What had I touched?

The bushes parted and a strange creature bounced out.

I had never seen anything like it.

It had the body of a dog, as big as a German shepherd, and the face of a squirrel.

I don't believe this! I thought.

It could talk, too. "In here! Quick!" the creature urged in a scratchy, squeaky voice.

Its squirrel-nose twitched. Its bushy dog tail thrashed from side to side.

Could we trust it?

"In here!" it squeaked.

It waved a paw in the air. Pointed to a bush of big orange leaves.

Pat held back, but I crept forward. I spotted the entrance to a cave hidden behind the leaves.

"It's a good hiding place," I told Pat.

"It's the Hiding Cave," the squirrel-dog announced. "The Hiding Cave is the place to hide. Quick!" The animal held the leaves aside for us.

The ground shook. I turned and saw furry blue beasts in the distance. They were moving quickly toward us.

"Better do it, Pat," I said.

Pat hesitated.

I yanked his hand and pulled him after me. I bent down to enter the Hiding Cave.

I suddenly remembered what happened when Nat touched the penalty rock. The thought made me shiver. Would we really be safe in the Hiding Cave?

Thump. Thump.

The beasts drew closer.

Pat hesitated and held back.

"Where are they?" a beast shouted. I recognized Fleg's voice.

"They must be nearby," Spork answered.

The squirrel-dog stayed outside. It let go of the orange leaves. They sprang back into place, hiding the entrance to the cave.

Pat and I crouched inside, hidden from view.

We huddled close together. The air felt damp inside. It had a sour smell that I tried to ignore.

I slumped against the wall of the cave and wiped the sweat off my forehead. I tucked my feet under me. "Try to get comfortable," I whispered to Pat. "We might be here for a long time."

Something tickled my neck. I reached to scratch it.

Something tickled my ear.

I shivered.

I brushed my hand against my ear and felt something crawl onto my cheek.

"Ow!" I cried out as I felt a sharp bite on my shoulder.

I turned to Pat. He was slapping at his ears and neck.

Something buzzed past my ear.

Something skittered through my hair. I shook my head hard.

My whole body itched and tingled. Every inch of me!

Beside me, Pat squirmed, and wriggled, scratched and slapped at himself.

I leaped to my feet. "Help!" I cried. "What is happening? What is going on in here?"

29

"Help!" I cried, scratching desperately. "Help us!"

The squirrel-dog's face poked into the entrance.

"What is happening to us?" I cried, squirming and scratching.

"I forgot to tell you," the strange creature whispered. "The Hiding Cave is also a hiding place for bugs!"

Bugs!

"Ohhh!" Pat let out a low moan. He rubbed his back against the cave wall. Scratched his hair.

The bugs were everywhere. Crawling on the walls. Flying through the air. Buzzing. Whistling. Clicking.

They crawled up and down my legs and arms. Over my face. In my hair.

I picked some kind of worm off my cheek. I dragged my hand down my arms and my bare legs, brushing bugs onto the cave floor.

Pat squirmed next to me. "Get them off me, Ginger," he wailed. "Helllp!"

"Sshhh!" The squirrel-dog stuck his nose back into the cave. "Quiet! Here comes the Beast from the East. Don't make a sound or he'll find you!"

Pat and I drew closer together.

I held my breath and tried not to move.

I counted to ten. Silently. I pretended there were no bugs on me.

I shut my eyes and pictured my bedroom. The posters on the wall. My comfortable canopy bed. I thought of being under the covers. Going to sleep.

And then I thought about bedbugs!

I couldn't ignore the insects crawling over me. It was impossible not to think about them.

I couldn't stand it. I needed to scratch. I needed to *scream*!

I couldn't sit there another second.

I heard a beast stomp close to the cave opening.

I recognized Spork's voice. "Hey — !" he snarled at the squirrel-dog. "Have you seen strangers here?"

Did Spork know this creature?

Were they friends?

"Answer me," Spork demanded.

I waited for the squirrel-dog's answer. Please don't tell them we're hiding in here, I prayed. Please.

A fat, wet bug landed on my face. I picked at

104

it with my fingers. It clung to my cheek. I pulled harder. I couldn't tug it loose.

I felt a scream building up inside me.

I couldn't take it another second.

My mouth opened.

I had to scream. I had to!

30

"Ah — "

I clamped my hand over my mouth.

I let out a tiny squeak.

The orange leaves rustled. Fleg's paw pushed into the cave entrance.

I froze. I heard Pat gasp.

"What's in there?" I heard Fleg ask the squirrel-dog.

"Bugs," the squirrel-dog replied. "Thousands of them."

Millions! I thought bitterly. The bugs crawled over my face, my arms, my legs. They buzzed in my ears.

Fleg pushed his nose into the cave.

I stopped breathing.

Fleg sniffed. "What's that awful smell?" he complained.

"Insects," I heard the squirrel-dog answer.

"They stink!" Fleg muttered. He let go of the leaves and they snapped back into place. "Only bugs in there," Fleg reported to Spork. "No humans."

"Of course not," the squirrel-dog said calmly. "The humans went the other way."

"Why didn't you say so?" Fleg exploded.

Spork shouted to the other beasts. "They're not here! The other way, quick! Only trel minutes left to play."

"I'll find her," I heard Spork tell the others. "I have to tag her back! No human is going to make *me* Beast from the East!"

I heard their footsteps pound in the other direction.

Only trel minutes! I didn't exactly know what trel meant. But I knew the game was nearly over. If Spork didn't tag me back, my brothers and I would be free!

But I couldn't take another second in this bug-infested cave.

I moved to the entrance on trembling legs. I itched so badly, I could barely control my muscles!

I peered out of the cave. "Are they all gone?" I whispered to the squirrel-dog.

"For now," he answered.

"Let's get out of here!" I called back to Pat. I sprang out of the cave. He jumped out after me.

We frantically brushed bugs off our skin and clothes. I scratched my head and rubbed my back up against a tree.

Pat stomped his feet. "They're even in my

boots!" he wailed. He untied his laces and pulled off his boot. He shook it upside down. A hundred black bugs poured onto the ground and scurried away.

"I'm never going to stop itching!" I wailed. "I'm going to itch for the rest of my life!"

"You'd better hide," the squirrel-dog warned. "They could be back. And you're only allowed to use the Hiding Cave once a game."

Pat and I thanked the strange creature. Then we plunged back into the woods.

I hadn't been in this part of the forest before. Pat and I pushed our way past a row of high bushes. I stopped.

A giant willow tree stood up ahead. Its branches spread low, sweeping against the ground.

The Gulla Willow?

It had to be.

I glanced around, searching for a hiding place. A long, low rock stretched beyond the tree.

Only a few minutes left.

"Quick," I whispered, grabbing Pat. I pulled him behind the rock.

"That must be the Gulla Willow," I told him. "When the sun sets behind it, we'll be safe."

Pat nodded but didn't reply. He was breathing hard. He scratched his cheeks. Still itchy. We were both still itchy.

"Stay down," I warned him. "And don't touch the rock."

We crouched together in silence.

And waited.

My heart slammed against my chest. My skin tingled. I huddled beside my brother — and listened.

Silence.

The whisper of the wind through the trees. No other sound.

"Are we safe now?" Pat asked in a trembling whisper.

"Not yet," I answered. I raised my eyes to the charcoal gray sky. A last ray of purple light spread over the top of the willow.

Hurry! I urged the sun. Go down! What are you waiting for?

The sky darkened. The purple light faded behind the Gulla Willow.

Only gray sky now. Night sky.

The sun was down.

"We're safe!" I cried, jumping to my feet. I turned and hugged Pat. "We're safe! We made it."

I stepped out from behind the rock.

A heavy hand slapped me hard. On the shoulder.

"You're It!" Spork bellowed. "You're the Beast from the East!"

31

"Huh?"

I gasped in shock. I could still feel the beast's stinging slap on my shoulder.

"No fair!" Pat cried. "No fair!" He stared as the beasts circled us. Pat had never seen them close-up before.

"It's dark! The sun is down!" I protested. "You can't tag me now!"

"Game Over! Game Over!" Fleg shouted. He stepped out of the woods and hurried toward the circle of beasts.

I pointed angrily at the Gulla Willow. "The sun set behind the tree. You can't tag me!"

"The game hadn't been called yet," Spork said calmly. "You know the rule. Fleg has to shout out 'Game Over' before the game can end."

The beasts all murmured agreement.

I clenched my fists. "But . . . but . . . " I stammered. I lowered my head in defeat. I knew they wouldn't listen to me.

Pat gulped. "What will they do now, Ginger?" he whispered softly. "Will they hurt us?"

"I already told you," I whispered back. "They're going to eat us."

Pat let out a cry. He started to say something. But there wasn't time.

Fleg stepped forward and grabbed me by the waist. He tossed me over his shoulder.

The blood rushed to my head and I felt dizzy. The ground was so far away!

Spork hoisted Pat over his shoulder.

"Hey — whoa!" I protested. "Put my brother down!"

"He was your Helper," Spork replied. "We always eat the Helper, too!"

"Put me down!" Pat shrieked. "Let me go."

But the huge beast ignored him.

They carried us both into a small clearing.

A large stone pit sat in the center. A raging fire burned inside the pit. Yellow and blue flames leaped at the sky.

Fleg lowered me onto a tree stump. Spork set Pat down beside me.

The beasts circled around us. Drooling. Licking their lips.

I thought I heard thunder. But I soon realized it was the sound of their stomachs growling.

"It's Flelday," Spork said, smiling. "On Flelday we always barbecue."

I swallowed hard. And stared at the flames leap-

111

ing against the sky. I wrapped my arms around my chest and hugged myself.

Spork poked at the fire with a long metal rod. He pointed the rod at me. "Yum yum." He grinned, rubbing his stomach.

I felt sick.

Gleeb lugged a huge pot over to the fire. He set it down in the middle of the flames.

Fleg pulled some gourds off the nearby trees. He cracked them open and poured their yellow juice into the pot. He collected sticks and leaves and tossed them in, too.

Gleeb stirred and stirred. A sour, rotting stench rose up from the pot.

"The broth is ready," Gleeb announced.

I turned to Pat. "I'm sorry," I said in a trembling voice. "Sorry I lost the game."

"I'm sorry, too," he whispered, his eyes on the flames.

The beasts began chanting. "Flelday. Flelday. Flelday."

"Who brought the barbecue sauce?" Spork asked. "I'm starving!"

Fleg lifted me in his arms. And carried me toward the cooking pot.

32

"Whoa! Wait! Stop!"

A familiar voice shouted across the clearing.

I jerked my head around. "Nat!" I screamed.

"Ginger!" Nat cried. He ran toward us, waving his arms. "What's going on? What are they doing?"

Fleg lowered me to the ground. "Nat — !" I screamed. "Run! Find help! Hurry!"

He stopped halfway across the clearing. "But, Ginger — "

"They'll eat you, too," I shrieked. "Run!"

"Capture him!" Spork shouted to the other beasts.

Gleeb and several others took off after Nat.

Nat spun around. He darted for the woods and disappeared into the trees.

I watched helplessly as the beasts plunged into the woods after him.

Don't find him, I prayed, crossing my fingers. All ten of them!

113

Nat will escape, I told myself. He'll climb a tree. He'll get away from them. Then he'll run and find help.

Pat and I stared at the dark trees. And waited.

"Oh, nooo!" I uttered a long wail when the beasts returned from the woods. And one of them carried Nat over his shoulder.

Nat kicked and punched. But he couldn't free himself.

The beast dumped Nat beside Pat and me. Nat landed hard, face-down on the ground.

Now they had all three of us. A feast!

Spork and Fleg gazed at us hungrily. Gleeb ran his tongue over his long fang.

I dropped down beside Nat. "How did you get out?" I asked him. "How did you get out of that cage?"

Nat rolled over and sat up. "It wasn't that hard," he said, groaning. "The boards were weak. I worked and worked — until I pushed enough boards out. Then I broke out."

"You should have stayed away," I told him. "You should have run. Now they're going to eat you, too."

Nat raised his eyes to the cook pot and the blazing fire. "I — I don't want to play anymore," he stammered.

"Nat," I whispered sadly, "I'm afraid the game is just about over."

33

"Quiet!" Fleg demanded. "Dinner — stop talking!" He stared at Nat.

Fleg's eyes narrowed. He tilted his head. He whispered to Spork and Gleeb.

The other beasts moved closer. They were all moving their eyes from Pat to Nat. They began murmuring to each other, shaking their big, furry heads. Their snouts waved up and down as they talked.

"You doubled!" Spork said to Pat. "You did a Classic Clone!"

I stared at the beasts. Studied their startled expressions. Hadn't they ever seen *twins* before?

"You doubled yourselves!" Fleg declared. "That's a Classic Clone. Why didn't you tell us?"

"Uh . . . tell you *what*?" I asked.

Fleg glared at me. "Why didn't you tell us that you are Level Three players?"

My brothers and I exchanged confused glances.

"You're in the wrong game," Spork announced, shaking his head.

"If you can double yourselves, that means you belong in Level Three," Fleg said. He slapped his furry forehead. "I'm so embarrassed! Why didn't you tell us sooner?"

"Well, I *told* you we didn't want to play," I replied sharply. "But you wouldn't listen."

"I'm so sorry," Fleg apologized. "We're only Level One players. We're just beginners. We're not experts like you."

"Experts?" Pat muttered. He turned to me and rolled his eyes.

"That's why we have to play in the daytime," Fleg explained. "We're not ready to play at night."

All around us, the beasts were muttering and shaking their heads.

"Of course, we'll have to let you go now," Fleg said. He scratched at his flabby chin.

"Well, of course," I cried. I wanted to jump up and down and shout for joy. But somehow I kept myself in control.

"That's it?" Nat cried to Fleg. "We're free?"

"Yes. Good-bye." Fleg scowled. He rubbed his belly. I heard it growl.

"Don't ask again," I told Nat. "Let's just get out of here!"

"Good-bye," Fleg repeated. He waved his paws as if he were trying to shoo us away.

116

I jumped to my feet. I didn't feel tired or scared or itchy or dirty anymore.

This time the game was really over!

"How do we find our parents?" I asked.

"That's easy," Fleg replied. "Follow that path." He pointed. "Follow it through the trees. It leads back to your world."

We shouted good-bye — and took off. The narrow dirt path twisted through the trees. Silvery moonlight danced over the ground.

"I am so glad you guys are twins!" I exclaimed.

I had *never* said that before! But I really meant it. They had saved our lives!

The trees thinned out. I could see a full moon climbing up over the dark treetops. I felt as if we were running to it, running into its warm, white light.

"Mom and Dad will never believe this story," I said. I planned to tell them every gory detail.

"They *have* to believe us," Pat declared. "It's all true."

I put on a burst of speed. My brothers ran harder to keep up with me.

I couldn't wait to get back. Mom and Dad must be so worried.

"Oh!" I gasped and skidded to a stop.

Pat and Nat stumbled into me. All three of us struggled to stay on our feet.

A huge beast had stepped out from behind a tree, blocking the path.

He crossed his furry arms over his enormous chest. His snout flared as he stared down at us with cold marble eyes. He opened his lips and growled, exposing his long fang.

I wasn't afraid. Not this time.

"Step aside," I ordered him. "You have to let us go by. My brothers and I are Level Three players."

"You're Level Three? Hey — that's great! So am I!" the beast exclaimed. "Tag! You're It."

ADD MORE Goosebumps®

TO YOUR COLLECTION...

HERE'S A CHILLING PREVIEW OF

THE CURSE OF CAMP COLD LAKE

I thought about my plan all the next morning. I was frightened — but I knew I had to go through with it.

Our group had Free Swim that afternoon. Of course, everyone had a buddy but me.

I dug my bare feet into the muddy shore and watched everyone pair up and head into the water. Puffy white clouds floated overhead, reflected in the nearly still water.

Tiny gnats jumped over the surface of the water. I stared at them, wondering why they didn't get wet.

"Sarah, it's swim time," Liz called. She hurried over to me. She wore a pink one-piece bathing suit under crisp white tennis shorts.

I adjusted my swimsuit top. My hands were trembling.

I really was scared by what I planned to do.

"Why aren't you swimming?" Liz demanded. She brushed a fly off my shoulder.

"I — I don't have a buddy," I stammered.

She glanced around, trying to find someone for me. But everyone was in the lake.

"Well . . ." Liz twisted her mouth fretfully. "Go ahead and swim by yourself. Stay close to the shore. And I'll keep an eye on you."

"Great. Thanks," I said. I smiled at her, then trotted enthusiastically to the edge of the water.

I didn't want her to guess that it wasn't going to be a normal swim for me. That I had something really terrible in mind. . . .

I stepped into the water.

Oooh. So cold.

A cloud rolled over the sun. The sky darkened, and the air grew colder.

My feet sank into the muddy bottom of the lake. Up ahead, I saw the gnats — hundreds of them — hopping on the water.

Yuck, I thought. Why do I have to swim with mud and gnats?

I took a deep breath and stepped out farther. When the cold water was nearly up to my waist, I lowered my body and started to swim.

I swam a few long laps. I needed to get used to the water. And I needed to get my breathing steady.

A short distance away, Briana and some other girls were having some kind of relay race. They were laughing and cheering. Having a great time.

They won't be laughing in a few minutes, I told myself bitterly.

A tall spray of water rushed over me. I cried out.

Another wave smacked my face.

It took me a few seconds to realize that I was being splashed — by Aaron.

He rose up in front of me — and spit a stream of water into my face.

"Yuck! How can you put this water in your mouth?" I cried, totally grossed out.

He laughed and splashed away to join his buddy.

He won't be laughing in a few minutes, either, I told myself. He'll treat me differently after today.

Everyone will.

I suddenly felt guilty. I should have told Aaron what I planned to do. I didn't really want to scare him. I wanted to scare everyone else.

But I knew if I told my plan to practical, sensible Aaron, he would talk me out of it. Or go tell Liz so that she would stop me.

Well . . . no one is going to stop me, I vowed.

Have you guessed my desperate plan?

It was really quite simple.

I planned to drown myself.

Well . . . not really.

I planned to dive down to the lake bottom. Stay under. A long, long time.

And make everyone think that I had drowned.

I can hold my breath for a very long time. It's because I play the flute. I've really developed my lung power.

I can probably stay underwater for two or three minutes.

Long enough to scare everyone to death.

Everyone will panic. Even Briana, Meg, and Jan.

Everyone will feel sorry for how mean they were to me.

I'll get a new start. After my close call in the lake, everyone in camp will want to be nice to me.

Everyone will want to be my buddy.

So . . . here goes.

I took one last look at all the laughing, shouting swimmers.

Then I sucked in the biggest breath I had ever taken.

And plunged down, down to the bottom of the lake.

The lake was shallow for only a few feet. Then the lake bottom gave way in a steep drop.

I kicked hard, pushing myself away from the other swimmers. Then I pulled myself upright, lowering my feet.

Yes.

I dropped my hands to my sides and let myself sink.

Down, down.

I opened my eyes as I dropped to the lake bottom. I saw only green. Waves of pale light shimmered through the green.

I'm floating inside an emerald, I thought. Floating down, down in a sparkling green jewel.

I pictured the tiny emerald on the ring Mom wore every day. Her engagement ring. I thought about Mom and Dad, thought how sad they'd be if I really did drown.

We never should have sent Sarah to that water sports camp, they would say.

My feet hit the soft lake floor.

A bubble of air escaped from my mouth. I pressed my lips tighter, holding the air inside.

I slowly floated up toward the surface.

I closed my eyes. I kept my whole body still to make it look as if I'd drowned.

I pictured the horror on Liz's face when she saw my body floating so still, floating under the water, my hair bobbing on the surface.

I almost laughed when I thought of Liz leaping into the lake to rescue me, having to get her crisp white tennis shorts wet.

I forced myself to remain still.

I shut my eyes even tighter. And thought about Briana, Meg, and Jan.

They'll feel so guilty. They'll never forgive themselves for the way they treated me.

After my close call, they'll see how mean they were. And they'll want to be best friends with me.

We'll all be best friends.

And we'll have a great summer together.

My chest began to feel tight. The back of my throat began to burn.

I opened my lips and let out a few more bubbles of air.

But my throat still burned, and so did my chest.

I floated facedown. I kept my legs stiff and let my arms hang loosely at my sides.

I listened for shouts of alarm.

Someone must have spotted me by now.

I listened for cries of help. For kids calling Liz.

But I heard only silence. The heavy silence you hear when you're underwater.

I let out another bubble of air.

My chest really hurt now. It felt about to explode.

I opened my eyes. Was anyone nearby? Was anyone coming to rescue me?

I saw only green.

Where is everyone? I wondered.

Liz must have spotted me by now. Why isn't she pulling me up out of the water?

I pictured her again in her white tennis shorts. I pictured her tanned arms and legs. I pictured her red hair.

Liz — where are you?

Liz — don't you see me drowning here? You said you'd keep an eye on me, remember?

I can't stay under much longer.

My chest is ready to explode. My whole body is tingling. Burning. My head feels about to pop open.

Can't anyone see me here?

A wave of dizziness swept over me.

I shut my eyes, but the dizziness didn't go away.

I pushed out the rest of the air in my lungs.

No air, I thought. No air left. . . .

My arms and legs ached.

My chest burned.

With my eyes closed, I saw bright yellow spots.

Dancing yellow lights. They grew brighter... brighter. They did a fast, furious dance all around me.

Around my burning, tingling body.

My chest ... exploding ... exploding ...

I'm so cold, I realized. Suddenly, I feel so cold.

The dancing, darting yellow lights grew brighter. Bright as spotlights. Bright as flashbulbs, flashing in my eyes.

Flashing around my still, cold body.

I shuddered from the cold.

Shuddered again.

Cold, thick water filled my mouth.

I've stayed under too long, I realized.

No one is coming. No one is coming to save me.

Too long ... too long.

I struggled to see. But the lights were too bright.

Can't see. Can't see.

I swallowed another mouthful of water.

Can't see. Can't breathe.

I can't stay under any longer. I can't wait any longer.

I struggled to raise my head out of the water. But it felt so heavy. It weighed a ton.

Can't stay down ...

Can't breathe.

With a burst of strength, I moved my shoulders. Pulled them up.

Hoisted up my head.

So heavy . . . so heavy. My hair filled with water. My hair so heavy. The water running down my face.

Over my eyes.

I turned to shore. Squinted through the bright, darting lights.

Squinted hard through the water running down my face.

Squinted . . .

No one there.

I turned again. My eyes searched the water.

No one there. No one swimming. No one on the shore.

Where is everyone? I wondered. Shivering. Shuddering.

Where did everyone go?

I struggled to shore.

My feet were numb. I couldn't feel the muddy bottom as I staggered out of the water.

I rubbed my arms. I couldn't feel the touch of my hands. Couldn't feel the water pouring off me, running down my back.

Couldn't feel anything. Numb. Numb all over.

"Where is everyone?" I called.

But did I make a sound? Did I have a voice?

I couldn't hear myself.

I stepped onto the grass and shook myself. Like a dog trying to get dry.

Trying to shake some feeling into my cold, numb body.

"Where did you all go?"

Hugging myself, I stumbled forward. I stopped when I saw the canoes. All tacked upside down by the shore and tied up.

Weren't kids canoeing today? Weren't the canoes all out in the lake?

"Hey!" I shouted.

But why couldn't I hear my shout?

"Where *is* everyone?"

No one on the shore.

I spun around, nearly losing my balance. No one in the water.

No one. No one anywhere.

I stumbled past the life preservers and rubber rafts. Covered with a canvas tarp.

Isn't anyone going to use them? I wondered. Why are they covered up?

Why did everyone leave the lake so quickly?

Shivering, hugging myself, I made my way toward the lodge. I gasped when I noticed the trees.

Bare. All winter bare.

"Noooooooo!" a frightened wail escaped my throat. A silent wail.

Could anyone hear me?

When had the leaves fallen? Why had they fallen in the middle of summer?

I started to trot along the path to the lodge. Cold. So cold.

Something stung my shoulder. Something tingled my eyelids.

Snow?

Yes. Tiny white flakes drifted down, blown by a steady breeze. The bare trees rattled and creaked.

I brushed snowflakes from my wet hair.

Snow?

But I knew that was impossible.

All impossible.

"Heeeeeeey!" My shout echoed through the trees. Or did it?

Could anyone hear my frightened call?

"Hellllllllllp!" I shouted. "Somebody helllllp me!"

Silence, except for the creaking tree limbs overhead.

I started to run again. My bare feet moved silently over the cold ground.

The cabins came into view as I made my way out of the trees. Their flat roofs were covered by a thin layer of snow.

The ground was as gray as the sky. The cabins were all dark, the shingled walls gray. Gray all around me.

A cold world of gray.

I pushed open the door of the first cabin I came to. "Hey — I need help!" I cried.

I stared into the empty room.

No one there. No camp trunks. No clothes scattered about.

I raised my eyes to the bunk beds against the wall. The blankets, the sheets — the mattresses — had all been taken away.

I guess this cabin isn't being used, I thought.

I backed out of the door. Turned and ran down the row of cabins. All dark and silent.

My cabin stood where the path curved up the

hill. With a sigh of relief, I ran up to it and pushed open the door.

"Briana? Meg?"

Empty. And dark.

The mattresses gone. The posters pulled down. No clothes. No bags or trunks.

No sign that anyone had ever lived in here.

"Where *are* you?" I shrieked.

And then, "Where am *I*?"

Where was my stuff? Where was my bed?

Uttering another terrified wail, I lurched out of the cabin.

Cold. So cold and numb. Running through the cold in my wet bathing suit.

I tore through the camp. Pulling open doors. Peering into bare, empty rooms. Calling. Calling for someone — anyone — to help me.

Into the main lodge. My cries echoing off the high, wooden rafters.

Or did they? Was I really making a sound?

Why couldn't I hear myself?

I burst into the mess hall. The long, wooden benches had been stacked on top of the tables. The kitchen stood dark and empty.

What has happened? I wondered, unable to stop my trembling.

Where did everyone go? Why did they all leave? How did they leave so quickly? How can it be snowing?

I stumbled back out into the gray cold. Wisps of gray fog floated low over the gray ground. I hugged my frozen body, trying to warm myself.

Terrified and confused, I wandered from building to building. I felt as if I were swimming again. Swimming in the thick gray mists. Swimming through endless layers of gray.

And then I stopped when I heard a voice.

A tiny voice. A girl's voice.

Singing.

She was singing in a high, frail voice.

"I'm not alone!" I cried.

I listened to her song. A sad song sung so softly.

And then I called out to her, "Where are you? I can't see you! Where are you?"

About the Author

R.L. Stine's books are read all over the world. So far, his books have sold more than 300 million copies, making him one of the most popular children's authors in history. Besides Goosebumps, R.L. Stine has written the teen series Fear Street, the funny series Rotten School, as well as the Mostly Ghostly series, The Nightmare Room series, and the two-book thriller *Dangerous Girls*. R.L. Stine lives in New York with his wife, Jane, and Minnie, his King Charles spaniel. You can learn more about him at www.RLStine.com.

HE SCARIEST PLACE ON EARTH!

EnterHorrorLand.com